Adele

CHANTE'S SONG

Enjoy!

Donneil D. Jackson

A NOVEL BY
DONNEIL JACKSON

ISBN-13: 978-0-9800311-0-2
ISBN-10: 0-0980031-0-9
Library of Congress Control Number: 2007942850

Pure Bliss Publishing
Newark, New Jersey
www.PureBlissPublishing.com

Printed in the United States of America

This is dedicated to my munchkinneck,
Kyler Dominique
I love you a whoooooooooooooooooooooooooooole
bunch!

Acknowledgements

This has been a long journey, years in the making, but Chante's Song is now a reality.

Thank you Lord! Thank you for the many blessings. Without you none of this would be possible. Please continue to give me strength.

I could not have been blessed with a better mother. Mommy, I love you to death. When I grow up I want to be just like you.

Kyler, thank you for being you. You know how to make Mommy smile in any situation just by batting your eyelashes and smiling at me. I never knew unconditional love until the day God blessed me with you. Thank you for being patient with me. (Note: you should be saying the same thing to me.)

People come into your life for a reason, season or a lifetime. To the people who have entered my life, served their purpose and moved on thank you for the contribution you made to my life. I wish you nothing but the best.

Certain people entered my life for a reason. Tayshia aka Tiesha, if we didn't spend our time writing about Vincent and Tyson I wouldn't have acknowledged the writer within me. Thank you, Carnetha, for being my friend in foreign land, for being interested in what I had written, and writing along with me. You became my new writing buddy. Karla Denise Baker, my motivator, every time I put the pen down you make me pick it back up. Thank you. Keep doing what you do to keep me on track.

There is a person who transitioned me from one phase of life to the next. Thank you for your support. I never knew support of your kind until I met you.

I can count all of my friends on one hand. Jamelia means beautiful. Your mother could not have selected a better name for such a beautiful person. Mabel, Joan has Lynn and Maya. You have me. My girlfriend (singing)! LaShaunna, my agree to disagree sister from another mother who is too much like me, we will always be Inspector Gadget and Sherlock Holmes. Shauntae, I love your free sprit, your determination, your strong willed self; I can do without the stubbornness. Yet all of those characteristics make you the beautiful woman that you are.

To the girl with the big hair, Dedra, my bestest friend in the whole wide world, remember the day we met 9th grade Ms. Delani's spanish class? We wouldn't become friends for another three years. It's strange the things we must experience in order for other things to occur. What we went through wasn't a good thing, yet I would do it all over again if it meant becoming your friend. I love you and will always support your decisions even when I don't agree. You already know I will be adding my two cents. You also know that… Sis-tah you've been on my mind, Sis-tah were two of a kind, Ohhhh Sis-tah I'm keeping my eyes on you… (In my Sug Avery voice).

Special thanks to Miriam Tager (my editor), everyone I forced to read Chante's Song fifty million times and give their opinions. Special thanks to Andre, Charmain (In life you choose your friends not your family, however you are one family member I would choose if given the option. I love you cuz), Debra, Desiree, Kai, Rachel, and all the authors I reached out to for help, advice, and suggestions on how we do what we do. To anyone I forgot to mention Thank you.

One

The sounds of Chante Moore's single "Chante's Got a Man" filled the bathroom. Vanilla-scented candles lined the tub while their aroma filtered the air. The bathroom was usually bright by day with all the sunlight that beamed through the floor to ceiling windows, but tonight the space was a reflection of the deep midnight-blue sky. I was truly feeling this song. My champagne glass swayed side to side to the melody of the music while the back scrubber served as a microphone.

"Chante's got a man at home." Those words kept ringing in my ears. You'd have thought I was in concert by the way I sang those lyrics.

The moonlight served as my spotlight. I rose as my audience clapped, winked at the reflection of this beautiful sister in the mirror, and then began to really blow. The words of Chante Moore floated out of my mouth like I was the songbird herself. Lord knows someone should give me a record deal. I laughed. I couldn't sing worth a lick, then again half of the singers out today couldn't sing either.

As the music faded, I retreated back to the sanctuary of my sunken tub. I added more hot water to maintain the same level of suds and the atmosphere. I pretended the bubbles surrounding me were the arms of Morris Chestnut. His sole purpose for being there was to please me of course. His body was the water, and I was submerged in it. His chocolate-covered fingertips stroked the back of my neck, sending chills down my spine while he planted kisses all over my breasts. He massaged my thighs and didn't stop until the tingling sensation reached my toes. I felt my thighs part. I gasped as he entered me.

Who in the hell was I fooling? I opened my eyes and reminded myself to cut this masturbation shit out.

Chante Moore and I did not have jack shit in common. Yeah, both of our names were Chante. And yeah, we were both beautiful, successful, black women. Might I add that I am more beautiful than she. However, she was Chante Moore, and I was Chante Chambers. She had a man, and I didn't. I believe that since "Chante's Got a Man" came out she's had two men. I haven't had a half of one.

Let us evaluate my list of lovers. It began with Jason McGee. If you could see Jason, you would drop your panties or slide those babies over to the side. He was gorgeous with a long tongue and large sex tool. Imagine the perfect shade of brown, nowhere near light, and not too far from being burned. He was that middle setting on the toaster oven when you want your bread just right. I could lick him from his goatee, up to his sideburns, across his wavy-haired head, and then back down again. Just thinking about his fine ass made me moist.

Picture this: 255 pounds of solid chocolate in the form of a football player, or a heavyweight boxer with the height of a basketball player. Sorry, but I cannot resist a handsome man with a muscular body, a lovable smile, a freaky inner self, and an exploring tongue. I forgot to mention dimples. Jason had two dimples that loved to call me. Jason was sexy as hell! If he knocked on my door right now and smiled that I-want-to-lick-you-all-night smile, I would gladly spread 'em.

Jason and I met in college and dated briefly. Back then our dates consisted of dinner, studying, and screwing, and not always in that order. Occasionally, we made it out to concerts and things of that nature. That was fine with me. After graduation he went his way, and I went mine. Three years later, guess who I bumped into at an industry event? None other than Mr. Sexy himself. We quickly became reacquainted. Let's just say some things never change. Somehow between talking business in a conference room at The W Hotel and reminiscing about old times, I ended up upstairs butt naked getting my freak on. Next thing I knew, I was leaving my job as head writer for *Sunset*, a soap opera, to go work for him at Jason World Productions. That was many years ago.

The four years that our relationship lasted were hell. I loved Jason with all my heart. I still did. The sex was magnificent. He was good at wining and dining a sistah. The only thing he couldn't master was keeping his dick to himself. How long could a woman play blind to her man's unfaithfulness? I must admit the shopping sprees and trips here and there kept me blinded for a minute. I was wifey. I had a diamond bigger than that rock Koby gave Vanessa to cover up his little indiscretion on my ring finger to prove it.

Jason had me sprung. While I was planning our wedding, writing screenplays, and producing damn near everything that crossed my desk, that dog was humping every female that opened her legs. The reason for his infidelities I never knew. Jason could have had me for breakfast, lunch, dinner, and even an afternoon snack. And he did. Wherever and however he wanted it, I was down. I guess that wasn't good enough. When it came down to Jason, all I saw was stupid! A dumb ass was what I was. I could have continued to sit back, play dumb to Jason's unfaithfulness, spend his money, and twirl my rock around my finger. However, when I walk into my man's office and see him laid back in his chair with some wanna-be-me bitch on her knees sucking his dick, it was time for me to open my eyes. That was it. I tried to do the mature thing. And I did.

"Fuck you, Jason," I screamed, walking out of his office.

Right after I walked out, I walked back in and threw my *Gucci* pump at the both of them. I felt relieved when it hit its intended target, the nasty-ass assistant I'd just hired. I looked like a damn fool as I limped down the hallway in one three-inch high heel. And so that's how Jason and Chante's love song ended.

It had been a year and a half since he last tasted my love. He calls every so often just to see how I am doing, and asks if I'd like to hang out with him, which is code for 'do you want to have sex.' He even asks if I need anything. Of course my response is always I am fine, I don't want to have sex with you, but there is this Dolce and Gabbana this, a Prada that or a Marc Jacobs something or other that had been calling me. Whatever Chante wants, Jason buys. He feels guilty and thinks that I am still bitter about the break up. To be honest, I was over that a year ago. But as long as he didn't know that, he would be eating out of my hand.

He loves me. I know he does. I love him, too. However, that is a feeling that I prefer to keep to myself. I had hope for us, yet I knew Jason was not ready for me. There would never be another episode of Jason and me. Frankly, he fucked up. I could not hang onto the arm of a man who the whole world knew cheated on me repeatedly. In my book, image was everything.

Presently, our relationship is weird. Jason is my boss, so it is strange. Occasionally we flirt. Mostly we, or at least I, try to keep it professional.

After Jason, I was like Toni Braxton singing, "Another Sad Love Song" until I met the New Jersey Jackals' star quarterback Curtis Thompson. Curtis was handsome. Built just the way I liked them. That Curtis could eat the hell out of an ass and fuck the shit out of your pussy. Lord knew his magic stick had me throbbing long after he was finished sharing his love. I had to rub myself for relief after he put it down. Our dates consisted of parties and publicity events.

Each and every time I wanted to be alone with him, he made up some excuse as to why he couldn't. At clubs I was ignored. But afterwards, it was my thick thighs he wanted to squeeze between. And just like a dummy, each and every time, I would let him. I had no problem with being his trophy woman in the daylight for publicity purposes and also the thighs he squeezed between at night, but I wanted a relationship. Curtis couldn't provide that.

After three months of dealing with Curtis and a month of being single, I fell for Shawn Eckford. I wasn't used to not getting my way, which was exactly what happened with Curtis. Shawn reminded me of Jason. He did everything in his power to please me. His sex was nothing to write home about, but I figured the basketball star was young. I'd just have to teach him a thing or two. And that I did. Our sex life improved and so did Shawn's appearance and popularity. As the relationship progressed, and his confidence increased, Shawn's interests and priorities changed.

Our quality time became less and less. PlayStation received more attention than I did. He began to let his hair grow. The one tattoo on his left arm was joined by some sort of design or phrase covering eighty-five percent of his body. Then came the bling bling. Lastly, the young boy from Tampa, Florida, traded me in for a bunch of niggas. Chante Chambers was second to no one! It was time for this approaching thirty-year-old woman to let the boy be a boy and find a man.

Then there was Derrick the photographer, who I allowed to take some nude pictures of me. Big f-ing mistake. The relationship was fine. I got the attention I craved. A few months into the relationship, I got a phone call from whom other than Derrick's wife. I was a lot of things, but homewrecker ain't one of them. Immediately, I broke it off.

That's when the drama began. Derrick didn't take rejection too well. My pictures started showing up any and everywhere. My mother received naked pictures of her daughter in the mail. And I had to explain to my brother why his little sister was butt naked in *Vixen* Magazine. My brother knew I looked good. But I could understand why he did not enjoy his friends getting a good look at his sister's ass.

Somehow, Jason managed to get a blown up black and white picture of me lying on my back with a sheet covering my essentials. It still hung in his home. I finally got the negatives and a formal apology on a billboard after my brother kicked Derrick's ass. I also got the last laugh after suing the crap out of him and the magazine for displaying my pictures without my permission. Ever since then I had a rule about dating photographers and taking butt naked pictures for anyone: never again would I drop my drawers for a camera. Nope, it wasn't going to happen.

Recently, Todd, a well-known rapper and I kicked it very briefly. Todd was into the limelight; I was the total opposite. To be the center of attention was a must for him. I preferred to be the center of his attention. He treated me like I was a trophy or something, like my only purpose was for him to show me off. I had been there before with Curtis and didn't care to go there again. We never spent time together just the two of us, and he never tried to put the moves on me, which I found odd.

All men tried something with me. I am not conceited. Yet, one must give credit where credit is due and this sistah was gorgeous! If Todd had an appearance to make, it was my fine ass on his arm. All night long, Todd referred to me as his fine-ass lady friend. I began to think "Fine Ass" was my nickname or something.

A few months ago, Todd had invited me to accompany him to some award show in LA and I agreed. I never past up a free trip or a reason to shop, just like Todd never past up an opportunity to have a beautiful woman on his arm. I wanted to be more than eye candy.

Todd shouted across the pressroom, "Yo, Chante, bring your fine ass over here and get in this picture."

Now how ghetto was that?

What really did it for me was when I laid across a king sized bed at the Beverly Hills Hilton, wearing a soft pink nightie that covered nothing. My coochie was begging for the year-long drought to end. Todd told me he was too tired to perform. *Son of a bitch!* I was tempted to ask him if he was gay. It was time to end the relationship, especially one that did not include sexual benefits.

Since Todd couldn't please me, I looked into pleasing myself. I went to toy parties and hosted a few. I met a few lovers there. That's where I met the *Everlasting Rabbit*. I had seen it on a *Sex and the City* episode. The loving was good. Too good to be honest. That's where I stood now. My boyfriend was a vibrator although right now we were not in agreement. I didn't agree with buying expensive batteries. Energizers could get costly. Consequently, once my bunny quit going, I placed him back in the drawer.

Lately, it had been Chante, Chante, and more of Chante. The last man's name I called was Jason's and that was over a year ago. One can see that I was horny as hell. I was sick and tired of being lonely. Chante was in search of something. I didn't know if it was sex or a steady relationship. Damn! Right about now I'd settle for a casual acquaintance. A companion. Someone I could call up and say, "Let's go to dinner," or "Hey, let's go see a movie," or "Let's get on a plane and go," or "Do you want to come over and fuck me all day long?" What man would turn that down? None.

I couldn't even convince myself. I did want more than sex. I wanted sex with real emotions behind it and not that sigh of relief after he busted a nut. I had been there, done that, and owned the damn t-shirt. Hell, I was the president of the getting screwed club. I wanted to come home to a man. I wanted a man to send me flowers just because. I wanted to know that there was a man out there who really loved me. I wanted my man to be my friend, to be patient with me, understand me, respect me and love me unconditionally. My man would kiss me, caress me, and send me off into ecstasy while whispering "I love you" into my ear. This mystery man would hold me, and work with me until I reached my big O. This guy would make love to every inch of my body and wash my feet like Jason did to Lyric in that movie. Every now and then, it would be okay for him to grab the back of my hair and fuck the shit out of me. I saw nothing wrong with that, just not all the time.

It took a special man to make love to you. I hadn't met him yet. I guess that was the reason why I had been celibate for the past year. I thought I had met that special man, but I guess the girl I caught between Jason's legs thought the same damn thing. I knew what I wanted, and it wasn't just sex.

I WANT A MAN! A RELATIONSHIP! I want to love and be loved. I would like to come home to a person instead of an empty condo that I paid too much money for. At night, I would actually like to go to sleep lying next to a man, as opposed to lying next to an empty spot. I wanted to be held. I hated watching TV by myself or dragging my best friend Kayla or my friends Tia, Yolanda, or Mecca to places I'd rather take a man. Most of all, I was tired of playing with myself.

As a beautiful black woman, my measurements were what many women would kill for or better yet pay for. I pampered myself on the regular. My hair hangs past my shoulders, and it's all mine. I get manicures and pedicures as part of my weekly maintenance. At least once a month, I frequent the spa. I have no children and a great paying job. Let me reword that I have a damn good career. I am capable of getting a date. I dated stockbrokers, lawyers, accountants, producers, writers, athletes, and doctors. You name them, and I have come close to fucking 'em. Yet, once the night came to an end, I was alone. Why was that?

At first I thought it was me. Maybe I came across as a bitch or something. However, after evaluating the dates, I realized that since I was not putting out they just weren't interested. I had a guy actually tell me that, after he asked me if he could screw me in one of the positions I had posed for in *Vixen* magazine.

When I go out and meet guys, the first thing out of their mouths was always something stupid. I couldn't walk down the street without some jackass asking "Weren't you in *Vixen*?" My reply was always, "No. I produced the movie *Sapphire*." Then they looked at me dumbfounded, so I asked "Do you watch TV? Ever seen *Best Friends*? I created that. The movie *Pride*, I produced that. Have you ever heard of Jason World Productions?" It's like everything I just said went in one ear and out the other because the dumbfounded look remained and the next comment was, "Would you get naked for my camera?"

At that point I was not even beat for the conversation. They all want to screw the bubbling brown bombshell that was bent over half naked in the magazine. It's like they expect me to be the dumb blond, or in this black girl's case, the dumb brunette. I guess they expect me to say, "Where your camera at, Daddy?" and begin taking my clothes off. Sorry, but Chante was not going to play dumb for a date. That was not going to happen!

Two

Enough of reliving the past, dwelling on what I want or didn't have. Tonight, I have a red carpet to grace. I should have invited Todd's handsome behind to accompany me to the premiere. I wonder how he would like it if I referred to him as my fine ass thug friend all night long? His conceited ass would probably love it. What the hell was his number?

"What's up, Todd?" I asked in an enticing voice.

"Hey, baby. What's your fine ass up to?" he responded.

"Well, right now, I am taking a bubble bath." I wanted him to imagine my fine ass naked, submerged in bubbles.

"Damn, Chante, you just put a good image in my head." I had him hooked. I felt a smile spread across his face. I wondered if my comment made his nature rise.

"I'm glad I did." What could I say? It's been a long time since I felt a man move inside me. Tonight I would give up on my hunt for a man; instead, I was in search of getting laid. I had big plans for Mr. Todd.

"Tonight I'm going to the premiere of *The Last One Standing*. Would you like to go with me?"

Todd would not pass up an opportunity to be seen in public with a beautiful woman on his arm, especially if the press was involved. He always made sure he smiled for every other camera and posed for those in between.

"I'm into something right now. But you know I could never pass up a chance to be with you. So what time does our date begin?"

Well at least I have a date, now. I was no longer in need of Kayla's cousin, Simone. *Thank the Lord! SHIT!* There was no time to call her and cancel; she called less than twenty minutes ago and said she was on her way. *Damn!*

Oh well. I guess it was going to be Todd, Simone, and me tonight. Todd would not have any problems with being in the company of two beautiful women. I guessed Simone's nickname would be beautiful bitch since I was his fine ass lady friend.

Returning to relaxation mode was harder than I thought. With closed eyes, I sank deeper into the tub, and accidentally wet my hair. Frizzy hair was the last thing I wanted or was it? The way I figured by the end of the night my hair would be frizzy anyway. I had the evening all planned out. The movie should be over around ten or eleven. We would eat dinner, ditch Simone, and by one o'clock in the morning I should be sweating up a storm and screaming, "Oh Todd! Oh Todd!" The thought made me smile.

That damn telephone always killed my thoughts. The Caller ID light flashed as the phone rang; I was reluctant to answer after checking the name of the caller. The phone rang another five times before I picked up.

"Hello, Franklin." It was the doorman informing me that my guest had arrived. He disturbed my bath and more importantly, he disturbed my thoughts of getting dicked down. Morris Chestnut was about to get back in the tub with me.

"Hello, Ms. Chambers. For a minute I didn't think you were in," he lied. That nosy man stalked me like a lion preying on food. "Your friend, Simone Atkins is downstairs. Would you like me to send her up?"

"Sure, Franklin." I hung up. He had more to say, I was sure of it. However, I did not feel like hearing it.

Franklin wanted me. He had asked me out once. And I kindly reported his ass to the building management. I wasn't that bad off, believe me if I were, he could catch it. But sistah girl would please herself until her fingers fell off before she showed Franklin the pimples on her ass.

"Why aren't you dressed?" Simone asked as soon as I opened the front door.

My hair was pinned up in a sexy up 'do. A hooded white terry cloth bathrobe covered my butt. I was clothed enough given the fact I just gotten out the tub. If she were a guy, it might have been sexy, despite the fact that the beady beads were starting to curl up. If it had been Jason at the door, I would not have made it into my sunken living room. Instead, Jason would have had a sistah butt naked doggie style on the top step. Or better yet, Curtis would have eaten me up right through the robe. I swear that man would always be number one when it came to tongue action.

"What's wrong with you?" Simone asked, staring at me like I was crazy.

"Nothing. I was just thinking about something. But hi to you, too." My thoughts of Jason and Curtis had me dazed for a minute and secretly rubbing my hot spot.

I followed Simone through my condo. Instead of walking straight into the living room to have a seat, she made a right to take a peek in my den. Then she kept straight, made a left and entered the living room, and walked through the dining room and stared at my view of the New York City skyline through the huge floor to ceiling windows in the living room.

"What are you looking for?" I asked confused.

She laughed. "A man. Do you have company?"

"No. And is there a reason you're looking for a man here?" Simone was one second away from being told to go home because now the girl was walking toward my bedroom.

"Look, I'm sorry if I interrupted your little masturbation session." She adopted an attitude. But then she must've remembered I had something she wanted, movie premiere tickets. "You said to be here by seven. And you're not dressed. Why do you have all these candles going?"

"Simone, walk yourself back into the living room, den, kitchen, wherever and wait for me." She was pissing me off.

Simone and I aren't what you call friends. She is my best friend Kayla's cousin. I hated the little heifer to be honest. It was something about her I just didn't trust. Kayla said I was jealous of the time she spent with Simone. She also said I was used to being the only eye candy when we went out. I must admit both statements were true. I didn't like sharing attention with anyone. But I didn't give a damn what Kayla said. I still didn't trust her slut of a cousin any farther than I could throw her.

I only agreed to bring Simone to the premiere because Kayla had begged me. I originally asked Kayla to go, but she had a prior engagement with her fiancé, Shawn. Or at least that was what she had told me. Once Kayla declined, I invited my girl Mecca. Kayla had bribed me with a pair of Manolos to take back my invite. I did. A sistah would do damn near anything for a pair of shoes, especially Manolos. Knowing Kayla the way I did, she probably just wanted to spend time with Shawn without being disturbed by her out of town, cock blocking cousin.

Simone was the biggest liar I had ever met. And believe me I have met some liars. Kayla and Simone had not seen each other since they were around fifteen years old. Fifteen years later right before her plane left Tampa, Simone called Kayla to ask if she could come visit. Kayla, being herself, agreed. Somewhere between staying a week and returning to the airport to go home, Simone remembered she'd only bought a one-way ticket.

She made up some excuse about being an actress and having a big audition. So Kayla agreed to let her stay. She did get that role. But I never knew people actually aspired to be porn stars. Three years later, she had worked her way up to shaking her ass in music videos. She was lucky enough to land the role of the main girl in two music videos. I believed the only reason she pretended to be interested in me was because I was HBIC at Jason World Productions. Translation: Head Bitch in Charge. In the words of 50 Cent, I run New York, or in my case, I ran Jason's World. If I wanted to make her a star, I could. After three years of knowing her, she should have realized that it wasn't going to happen.

"Damn, baby, your fine ass is looking good!" Todd really

knew how to complement a lady.

"Thank you, Todd." I smiled because I knew I was looking great in my silk burnt orange shirt/dress. I wasn't sure if it was a dress or shirt. It wasn't long enough to classify as a dress, and it was a tad too long to be a shirt. The long sleeve shirt/dress was not tight, yet it clung to me just the way it should. The silver trimming that traced the end of the sleeves also lined the slit in the front. The slit revealed enough cleavage to show the firmness and shape of my 36C's. I was unsure if my booty would be hanging out, so my shirt/dress was accompanied by matching boy cut briefs. My french manicured toes accented my silver sandals. A sistah was looking HOT!

Todd looked very handsome in a black suit. A black fedora was his only accessory. I expected him to show up in a pair of jeans with a polo shirt and some Timberlands. It wouldn't have mattered because the film's director, T.J. Hampton, had on some army pants. His wife was another story. Can you say swap meet? Todd showed some class. He gained five 'I might get my dick sucked' points tonight. If he made it to twenty-five, by the end of the night he would get some head. I might even swallow.

Ha Ha Ha! I laughed out loud at that one; I wasn't going to swallow shit. I was a lady. I didn't do things like that. I chuckled at that lie.

Simone smiled through gritted teeth at Todd's comments to me; she was jealous. The look in her eyes told me to watch her. She wore a simple black asymmetric Dolce & Gabbana dress. Although she looked simple, plain Jane-ish, not her normal whorish looking self, she looked cute. I'm one to playa hate, but the outfit had Kayla written all over it.

Kayla was so plain Jane, and Simone was the total opposite. She was eccentric and liked to show tits and ass. She dyed her jet-black hair blond and wore it curly. I must admit the new color fit her since she was so light. Her makeup was calm; normally it was loud and all over the place. Her black strappy sandals were bad. Simone was definitely competition for the night. If she batted her eyes over here one more time, I was going to smack her to the other side of the street.

"You look good, too, Baby." Todd was referring to Simone.

The girl was cheesing so hard I thought her face would bust.

"You look good, too," Simone said, "but you look like you would feel more comfortable in some jeans and some Tims."

"Yeah, I would, but you can't wear jeans and boots everywhere." Todd just earned two more points.

I ended their conversation quick. Todd was my screw; Simone had better lay her eyes on someone else. I knew that if Todd was not with me, he would have tried to talk to Simone. Todd, like so many of our black brothers, was a fan of the high yellow heifers. When he first approached me, I questioned why he wanted some bubbling brown sugar, like myself, and he had said, "Chante, ya chocolate butt is sexy as hell." I was still not sure if he was referring to my picture in *Vixen*, since there was a picture of me covered in chocolate, or me in the flesh.

Snap. Snap. As soon as my sandal touched the red carpet, the cameras began to snap. I heard "Oh's" and "Ah's" coming from all directions. I even heard the, "No she didn't's." The press stood behind a barricade along with the fans, who were out in huge numbers. Questions came from all directions. There were questions about my dress. Questions about my date. Questions about the film and the cast.

"Who are you wearing?" Kaitlyn Monroe, from *Style Magazine* asked.

"Mia Tyler Couture," I responded. A Kool-Aid smile sat on my face as I began my journey down the red carpet with Todd on my arm. I was working the hell out of the red carpet and I looked damn good doing it. The looks of awe on the faces of the crowd reassured my feelings. I pushed Todd aside a few times to model my shirt/dress. I knew he didn't like that because he was a camera hog, and I was taking up too much of the photographers' film.

"Smile," I said and pulled Todd closer to me as I posed for the camera. Todd as usual was right on cue; he just earned two more points.

Todd looked at me. He must have been reading my mind, the next thing I knew his lips were all over mine. Snap. Snap. Snap. The paparazzi and every person with a camera began taking our picture. Afterwards, every reporter had a question.

"Chante, is this your way of telling the public that you and Todd are a couple?" Jacqueline Grant, the host of *Celebrity Sightings* asked.

The kiss had me speechless. I was too busy calculating how many dick-sucking points Todd had earned. The way I figured it, he just earned ten more points. I just smiled and kept on walking down the red carpet. Todd, on the other hand, had words for the world.

"We are not a couple." He winked at me. "We're *really* good friends." He emphasized the word *really*. Todd smiled and posed some more for the camera.

Oh, really. Later on we will see just how good of friends we are. I grinned.

As I entered the theater, I turned my head around to see where Simone was, and whose eyes were glued on me? Mr. Jason McGee. *Damn, that man is gorgeous!* His eyes were telling me I looked good enough to eat. His balled fist told me he did not appreciate the kiss Todd had just laid on me. I winked at Jason as I spoke with Black Entertainment Television. As I turned back around, I noticed Simone's eyes were on Jason.

Oh, no, Boo Boo, that was a big no no. Jason would always be my man. I was too pretty to have a catfight, but I gave myself a mental reminder to have a talk with Miss Simone.

Inside the lobby, I was sure to get in a few pictures with Jason. I purposely brushed my breast all over his white suit.

"What are you doing?" he asked staring at my cleavage.

"I think you should tell me what you're doing because I'm smiling for the camera. So, uh…I think you should *look* at the camera instead of at my breasts." I repositioned myself, thrusting my apple bottom into his pelvis harder.

"How about you dump your little date, and we ditch the premiere and I handle that," he whispered in my ear.

One quality I loved in Jason was the freak in him. He was so spontaneous. On many occasions, we frequented bathroom stalls for a quickie when we should have been doing other things. I wanted to say, *Hell yeah, baby, you could catch it,* but I was looking too good to be anyone's quickie.

"Jason, by the way how's the cheap slut I caught sucking your dick? What was her name? Was it Keisha, or Teresa? Or was it Lisa or Kim?" I had to remind Mr. McGee why we were not together anymore. I left Jason's side, on my way to scoop my date up from Simone's clutches.

Jason grabbed my arm and whispered in my ear, "You might want to turn your high beams off." He laughed and walked away to find his tramp for the night.

My nipples were just the way I wanted them, erect. Not!

By the time the movie was over, I thought my nipples were going to explode. I knew my silk boy cut briefs were damp. I wanted to skip dinner and just let my love come down all over Jason in the limo. *Damn! Why was that man on my mind so hard?* All movie long, he played with my spots. Somehow, we were seated together, which I didn't mind. Jason kept running his fingers down my neck and blowing in my ear. Once or twice his tongue caressed my earlobe.

Every time Todd glanced over at me, I would laugh like something in the movie was funny. In all actuality I was laughing because Jason was whispering in my ear how much he would love to wrap his lips around my voluptuous breast. If he wasn't saying anything he was licking my ear or kissing my neck. *DAMN! He knows that's my spot.* I didn't know what had come over Jason. We had been known to flirt, but tonight Jason was all action. He had not touched me in a sexual way since our last encounter.

Was it the Mia Tyler ensemble that was turning him on?

Jason always said I looked good in that color. Was it the fact that I was looking gorgeous? Oh hell no. I looked good even on my bummy days. Was it my cleavage? Jason had always been a breast man; he sucked a titty like he was a breastfed baby.

"Do you wanna head over to Amy Ruth's in Harlem?" Todd interrupted my thoughts. "The collard greens are banging."

"Let's go to the Roxy," chimed in Simone.

"How about we go back to my place?" I was horny and didn't have time for playing games or beating around the bush. I could've just said 'Todd do you wanna fuck my fine ass,' but I was looking too pretty to have such a raunchy mouth. "I have this new blender, and I've been dying to make some margaritas." *Yeah, right! I didn't want to sound like a slut.*

"That's cool." Todd wanted me as much as I wanted him. While Jason was locating my hot spots, Todd kept on rubbing my thigh, each time he got closer and closer to my honey pot.

"I thought we were going out to eat. I didn't eat anything for that reason," Simone whined.

I felt like saying, 'Look bitch, would you like it if we dropped you off at McDonald's?'

"Simone," I said, "the Roxy is a club."

"Well, can we stop and eat?" She rolled her eyes. "I'm hungry."

I rolled my eyes right back at her. "Simone, when you get in the house you can eat whatever you like."

Once we pulled up in front of Kayla's house, Simone

acted as if she couldn't find her keys. To make matters worse, Kayla conveniently did not answer the door or her telephone.

"Can you please park here for a moment?" I asked the driver. I kept pressing redial on my Blackberry because Kayla was going to stop whatever she was doing, get her butt up, and open that door.

"Are you sure you don't have your keys?" Todd asked. He was becoming annoyed as well. He had just earned himself a blow job. "Won't you check your purse again?"

After pressing redial about ten more times, Kayla finally answered the phone. If she hadn't answered I was going to have the driver beep the horn. At midnight, in her neighborhood, her neighbors would have called the police for sure.

"Hello." She tried to sound asleep. I would bet money that neither she nor Shawn was sleeping.

"Sorry to interrupt your escapade, but your cock-blocking cousin is back. You might want to open the door." If she hadn't opened the door, I really didn't care. Simone was getting out of the limo.

♫

Before we were completely out of the driveway, my briefs were off, my thong was to the side, and Todd was tasting my love. My love fell down as soon as his tongue flickered over my clit. It had been a long time. The driver had to hear my moans even though the partition was up. I had orgasm after orgasm, riding down the hill. A sistah was ready to explode. He earned himself a blowjob, and I gave it to him. I was never a selfish lover. After awhile I could no longer take the excitement. Looking Todd dead in his eyes, I removed my thong, and prepared him for impact. I never screwed without protection. I wiped my knees after being on the floor of the limo and progressed to working up a sweat.

My plan was to ride Todd all the way down South Orange Avenue, from Livingston to South Orange, which was not a long ride at all. My intentions were to sweat out my up 'do hairstyle. However Todd's malfunction caused me not to be able to follow through with my plan. Let's just say Todd's train was not the little engine saying 'I think I can, I think I can.' He was saying I can't. His car ran out of gas and oil, too.

Ain't that a bitch!

Three

I failed at getting laid. I guess it wasn't meant for me to get my itch scratched. The rabbit was calling me as I lay in bed. *Chante...Chante...put some batteries in me.* I tried to fight the urge, but I could not. As I searched through my toy drawer, I decided against the Rabbit and grabbed my Baby Boy. The packaging guaranteed an orgasm in less than five minutes. *GODDAMNIT!* I could not pop the purple toy open to put the batteries in. It was going to be the Rabbit and me. I reached over and took the batteries out of the television remote control. To my dismay, the batteries were not a match.

Goddamnit! My foot was in pain after walking straight into one of the metal legs on the hall table, all in the name of a fix. No time to rub my foot. I could have kicked Todd's ass. My foot was hurting like hell. I was a coke fiend searching for a straw, the way I went through my kitchen drawers looking for size C batteries. Was it really worth it? Yeah it was worth it! I couldn't believe that little bastard licked my kitty cat like it was going out of style and then had the nerve to stop short on me. I had actually given him some deep throat action, and that was how he did me?

Maybe he had a hard on for a while, and that was why he came so soon. I thought about that. So I attempted to give him the benefit of the doubt. After the little engine conked out, I proceeded to give him a professional job just to get him going again. And what happened? There is no need to even say. If sex had happened, I wouldn't be searching for batteries to fuck myself.

By the time I was finished going through every drawer in the kitchen, I had a pile of shit on the floor. Operation Find Batteries was a failure. The best thing I could do for myself right now was to take a long hot shower and hope the tingly feeling went away.

As the hot water hit my breast, I felt Jason's tongue kissing and caressing my neck. The kissing moved down to my breast. As the water massaged my back, Jason played with my front. His fingers played hide and seek in my love palace while his thumb ran in a circular motion around my home base. The warmth of his mouth grew closer to my entrance. My hands served as a guide to the land of the lilies. My breathing grew rapidly, my heartbeat pounded, and my hands dug deeper into the valley. Nectar began to ooze out. Lips quivered while my legs shook. My eyes opened and I was alone.

My heartbeat returned to normal, and my breathing became steady. There was a melody in my head, and I just couldn't shake it. I couldn't remember the name of the song, but I knew it was T-Boz from TLC singing it. The song was about touching one's self and it being alright. Was it alright for me to touch myself? I believed that saying 'when you don't have a man you always have your hand.'

Up until that night, I had never questioned that theory. Nevertheless, if it were really alright I could've just played with my clit in the limo when Todd went limp on me, not once, but twice. I could have said, "Oh, excuse me, Todd, you don't mind, do you?" But no. I sat back with a tight lip and remained quiet.

Whether it was all right or not to touch myself, I didn't give a damn. In the middle of my king size sleigh bed, with open vertical blinds, I laid butt naked, for all to see. It felt great as my fingers ran across my privates. It didn't take long for the panting, quivering, and heart pounding to begin. Once it did, I invited it to come back again, just to let all the backed up love come down.

All the touching and rubbing that I was doing was nothing compared to being with a man. My clitoris was enjoying the self-pleasuring, yet my vagina demanded for something to be inside of her. My finger was not it. I was tempted to call Jason. He would pull out of whatever whore he was in to feel the walls of my tunnel. All I had to do was make the call. I glanced over at the telephone sitting on my nightstand. The booty call would be well worth it, on both parts. I was sure of it. I picked up the phone. Was I that desperate to call upon my ex?

Hell yes! I began to dial his number. The thought of Jason being inside of me made me tingle and smile. Did I really want to call him?

Hell no! A sistah had too much pride. I rolled over, placed the cordless back into its cradle, and called it a night.

Fuck it! I stuck my pride in the drawer next to the Rabbit and picked up the phone.

"What up?" he answered after two rings.

"Jason, where are you?"

Wherever he was it was very noisy.

"At the Roxy. Why? What's up?"

"I called you because…" I proceeded to beat around the bush to get to the nature of my call. Jason appeared to be preoccupied. His *uh mums* changed to long drawn out *uh mums*.

"Jason, what are you doing?" I began to question the sounds I was hearing. It sounded like a coke bottle being suctioned.

The look on my face turned to disgust. What really caused a frown was when I heard a soft feminine voice ask if he liked it and wanted more. Then the same voice asked him if he wanted her to swallow.

I just hung up.

That's what I get. I knew I was going to regret making that phone call. How dare he allow me to hear that! Did he want me to know that someone was sucking his dick? Was he throwing it in my face that it could have been me? Why didn't he give me enough respect to say 'I'll call you back?' The tingly feeling quickly faded away as I continued to analyze what had just happened. I went from feeling mad, to disrespected, to disgusted, to just plain ole hurt. The only wetness that remained was the tears rolling down my face.

Four

Two weeks and too many phone calls later, I was still dodging Todd. He should've gotten the hint when I left his ass standing outside the limo. But he proceeded to follow me into my building. He should have been embarrassed after his little willie went limp on a sistah. He didn't seem to be since he entered the elevator with me and followed me upstairs to my apartment. Did he really think the offer to taste my margarita was still on the table? *Whatever!* I smiled, kissed his forehead and left his ass standing on the other side of my closed door.

At first I was too pissed with Todd to speak to him. I sucked his dick for nothing. As a lady you don't suck every guy you meet. Hell, I did it twice, and what did it equate to? Not a damn thing. It was because of him I was forced to touch myself. And I was forced to call the man whom I love and listen to some ditsy bitch lick his lollipop. To be honest, I got over that quickly when a Birken bag and Giuseppe shoes were delivered to my office courtesy of my *Daddy*, Jason. Yet, every time I thought of some woman sucking Jason's dick I had flashbacks. Then I got more and more pissed off.

I didn't know why Todd was still calling. The day after his accident, he called and apologized on my answering machine. That was fine. He even asked me out again. Of course I did not return that call. I could not guarantee that the next time I would just sit back and say nothing. Then he called again. And again. Did he think I was going to allow him to explain? No explanation was needed. I understood perfectly. He was not capable of keeping an erection; one nut and he was done. I see why I had been rejected in LA. The other night he tried to conquer the throne and was defeated.

If he really wanted another chance, he should've sent me a gift. Didn't he get the memo? Chante Chambers can be bought.

I did not tell a soul about my short-lived rendezvous in the limo. I tried to tell Kayla, but as soon as she heard my voice on the other end of the phone she cursed me out for bringing Simone home early. After she brought me up to date with her ruined night of romance, I just hung up.

In addition to me dodging Todd, Jason was trying his best to avoid me. I knew he felt guilty about that phone call and that's why he had bought me the bag and the shoes. Jason was good at buying gifts when he did something wrong.

One day last week we saw each other in passing, and he quickly entered the elevator. No, 'Hi, Tae Tae, did you get the bag and shoes?' or anything. He didn't even smile. I believed he knew why I called him. I also believed he thought Todd and I had sex. If only he knew what I knew.

The red blinking light on my desk phone advised me that I had a message. This distracted me from watching my talk show. I didn't know what was more distracting, the flashing light or the gold teeth of some girl's alleged baby daddy. One or the other had to stop. I had no control over Goldie on the television; however, I could make the flashing light stop.

There was a message from Jason.

"When you get this message, come upstairs. I need to speak to you." I pressed number one, to replay the message just to hear his voice again.

I hung up after being advised that there were no more messages. *What? No calls from Todd?* I was shocked. He had been blowing up my house phone, office phone and cell phone. Actually, I had been Todd free for the past few days. Finally, he had gotten the hint. *Hallelujah. Hallelujah.*

Now what could Jason possibly want at ten in the morning? Didn't he know I was not to be disturbed during *Maury?* I loved the paternity test shows. I could've sworn I sent out an email telling everyone not to bother me between the hours of ten and eleven, and twelve and one. I turned my eyes away from the flat screen television hanging on the wall and admired Times Square. I needed to figure out what could have been so important to stop Jason from avoiding me.

His voice had not sound inviting on the message. As a matter of fact, it sounded demanding. The more I analyzed his voice, the more it turned me on. My insides began to tingle. I wasn't quite sure if it was Jason's voice that made me tingle or if I was having aftershocks caused by my morning encounter with the Baby Boy.

I couldn't believe I was missing Maury Povich for this shit. For the past ten minutes, I had been sitting across from Jason as he yelled and rambled on about and I quote, "motherfuckers complaining about the script." The motherfucker in question was Todd.

"Motherfuckers are saying that for you to be the executive producer, you ain't doing your job. You are not satisfying their needs."

From the time Jason had started speaking, my attention had gone out the window and landed on Broadway. My eyes surveyed the numerous billboards. I had never actually seen Jason's view of Broadway. I mean I had seen it, but had not really paid attention to it. That day, staring at Broadway seemed more exciting then listening to Jason go on and on.

Finally, he shut up.

"Good morning to you, too, Jason," I said, smiling. "I don't recall sleeping with you last night." *I would have loved to though.*

Jason grinned. It was not because of my smile; he was staring at my cleavage.

"Tae Tae," he snapped out of his trance. I wondered if he was thinking what I was thinking.

During the sixty seconds of silence, I saw my sheer crème blouse drop to the carpeted floor and my bra land on Jason's desk while my breasts were in his mouth. The thought made me tingle. I readjusted my blouse and played with the pink beads that lined the keyhole in the center.

"Do you hear me talking to you?" Jason asked.

Honestly, I was too busy daydreaming about making love to the fine specimen who sat in front of me.

"Yeah, I hear you." It was in my nature to give Jason attitude.

"I don't know what happened between you and Todd.

Personally I don't give a fuck. All I know is that at first he loved everything and now he hates it. I don't give a damn how you do it, just make the shit right."

"Jason, what the hell are you…"

"Shut up and listen!"

I knew he had lost his damn mind when he told me to shut up. From that point on, I certainly wasn't listening. Nor, was I fantasizing about him. Once again my attention was on Broadway. Gap had a new billboard. I heard Jason say something about how my relationship with Todd was holding up production. He was unable to pay the crew to show up to do a job if the talent wouldn't even show. He was trying to make money and I was fucking it up. Todd's scenes should have been finished today, and it hadn't even gotten started. Now other scenes couldn't be shot because he was in them.

"I don't like people trying to go over your head and come to me with bullshit based upon something personal."

I smiled.

He continued. "Even if it was business related, I don't have time to deal with the cats you fucking. You coulda rode daddy's dick, but no, you wanted to go play with that fake ass thug. And look at him crying to ya boss probably cuz you didn't suck his dick. Nah. I raised you. You sucked that nigga's dick. And I know you did a good job. He wanted you to swallow?"

"Jason, are you finished?" Jason was getting too goddamn personal for me.

I guess he wasn't finished because he kept on talking. It was enough for me. I stood, pulled the wedge out of my butt, and walked out of his office.

"Rosemary?" As soon as I walked back into my office, I buzzed my assistant.

"Yes, Chante?"

"Can you come into my office for a moment?" My nosy assistant would know if something were up. Rosemary was gossip queen.

"I know you and Doris talk from time to time." Hell, everyone knew they gossiped together every day. I would bet fifty dollars as soon as she walked out of my office she would be calling up to the 38th floor to gossip about me calling her into my office. "Have you heard anything about Todd complaining to Jason about me?"

A wide smile spread across Rosemary's face, and I knew I had gone too far. I should have made other arrangements to find out what was going on.

Rosemary sat down across from my desk, crossed her legs, and began to speak.

"From what I hear, Todd told Jason that he couldn't continue to do business with Jason's World if you worked here. He threatened to let *Bigs* produce his next music video and the rest following. He never actually told Jason why.

"He just said that you and he did not see eye to eye. That you didn't cater to his needs. Todd asked Delia to change the script. She told Todd that before she could make major changes she would have to run them by you." She crossed her legs to the other side and sipped her tea.

"Do you remember last week, when I told you Delia wanted to make some changes to the script?" she asked.

I nodded. I did remember that. There was no need in changing something that I had already put my stamp of approval on, nor was there any time to make drastic changes to a script that had two episodes surrounding it. There was nothing wrong with my concept. Todd's Character, Killa was going to die in episode twelve. If he kept fucking with me I would make some drastic changes and kill his ass in episode ten.

"Well, Delia told Todd you said no. Since then, from what I hear, Todd has been on the phone trying to get Jason to change everything from you being the executive producer, to Michael being the producer, to Delia being the director, down to Sandra and the rest of the writers.

"I also heard Todd went as far as trying to talk to some of the bigwigs over there at *Showtime*. Jason shut that down quickly. Jason said he's not changing shit for that fag. Chante, those were Jason's words not mine. Jason said if you said no it was for a reason, and he personally didn't want to get in it with you over that."

"Girl, you got Jason whooped." Rosemary reached across my desk and slapped my arm. She needed to keep that comment and slap to herself. She was no girlfriend of mine, and I didn't want her to think she was.

"Excuse me?" I gave her the 'we are not cool' look.

"I'm sorry, Chante." She looked down. "For the past two days, Todd hasn't been on set. Prior to that, he was calling you like crazy. When you told me to tell him to stop calling and throw his messages in the garbage, I assumed it was over the script."

Rosemary thought she was slick trying to get gossip out of me on why Todd was calling me. Once again I gave her the 'mind your damn business' stare.

"You shouldn't assume anything." I cut my eyes at her. "What the hell is wrong with the script?"

"I don't know."

For once Rosemary didn't know something. I was shocked.

"Doris says these last two days have been hell on her because Jason is pissed. You know how he is when it comes to spending money."

No, I didn't know how he was when it came to spending money. I got everything I wanted from him without complaint. I made a mental note to get those sandals Kimora Lee Simmons was wearing on a Baby Phat billboard.

"Get Todd's manager on the phone."

Rosemary stood and walked toward the door.

"Thank you very much, Rosemary."

A few minutes later, Rosemary buzzed me to inform me that she had Todd's manager on the phone.

After threatening Todd through his manager to make sure his client brought his ass to the set the next day and accepted the fact that his character died or he would have to pay back the advance and bonus he received, I knew my point was made. I never negotiated with creativity, especially not after everything had been arranged and production had begun. I also could not negotiate with a man whose dick couldn't stay hard. Tyree Wallace, Todd's brother, also known as his manager, knew I wasn't playing.

When I hung up, I heard him mumble the word bitch. That was okay because I knew Todd would be on set the next day.

Everything made sense. Jason felt bad because I heard some whore giving him a blowjob. That was the reason why he was avoiding me. Todd, on the other hand, was stalking me because he didn't want me to tell a soul that he was a one-minute hump. But, what would I look like if I told others that I had wasted my time, mouth and crotch on a one-minute fuck? Like a damn fool! So to get rid of me, Todd began this song and dance because his character died.

When he first had signed on, it was for twelve episodes. Showtime brought back our hot new miniseries, *On the Block*, for two more seasons. He had known that after the first season, his character wasn't coming back. Since I wanted to screw his sexy ass, I did some things to work Killa into the plot, but he knew Killa wasn't going to be around for much of season two. He had signed a contract and graciously accepted his bonus for renewing the contract, on an episode by episode basis. There was no point in acting like a bitch now.

And what would happen if this piece of information was leaked to his fans? How would they react if they knew he couldn't hang? He was known to have a magic stick that would go for hours. He would definitely lose the majority of his fans, which were women. His raunchy lyrics had women begging for just one night with Mr. Luva Luva. Anyone not exposed to his music, damn sure wanted a piece of his sexy ass after seeing him on *On the Block*. I knew my panties were moist after watching him slay his girl, Asia, last Wednesday night.

Did he really think Jason would silence me? Todd must have been out of his freaking mind when he thought Jason would kick me to the curb in order to satisfy him. He was trying to ruin my name. If he would have just sat back and took the rejection, no one would have known his little secret. But since he tried to go against me, he had to deal with me. That one-minute humper was going to feel the wrath of Chante Chambers.

Five

"Blazing 99," someone finally answered the station's hotline after about a million rings.

"Can I speak with Kayla, please?" I asked.

"Who can I say is calling?"

"Chante Chambers."

"Hey, Tae Tae," Kayla spoke into the phone.

"What up, Ma," I said in my loud ghetto girl voice.

"You are so ghetto."

We laughed.

"You should speak, Miss I can't come to the door because I'm fucking."

"What's so important that you are calling me on the hotline? I'm still mad at you about that night. Are you canceling girl's day at the spa? If so I am not allowing you to. I will be at your job in about thirty minutes."

"No, I am not canceling the spa. My body is in need of a massage." To be honest, I had forgotten all about our trip to the spa. "I know you are not still mad at me because I interrupted your living room rendezvous. I could imagine Shawn's face when Simone walked through your little love nest. Didn't you say he had whipped cream and strawberries all over his dick?

"What kinda shit are you two into? I can see it right now, with the fireplace going in 80-degree weather. Champagne glasses filled with some Hypnotic, and you with whipped cream and chocolate all over your tits."

I busted out laughing.

Kayla began to whisper. "Why'd you bring Simone home so early? You could've kept that girl out later or took her home with you."

"And you could've asked her to join in. I know Shawn would've really loved that. Besides I wanted to get my freak on, too."

"With who? A battery operated appliance?" She laughed.

"Heifer, don't knock it 'til you try it. I had a fella in the limo."

"Okay, now we are getting to the purpose of your call. But how about I call you right back from my cell phone because I am about to leave?"

"Fine! Just hurry up because sistah girl has gossip." The word gossip sang out of my mouth like opera.

Kayla never called me back; instead, within thirty-five minutes she was sitting across from me in my office with a Kool-Aid smile on her face. I was not sure if the thought of gossip caused the smile or if she was happy I finally got some.

"Well," she said still smiling.

"Well, what?" I asked. My smile matched hers.

"So tell me about this fella you had in the limo." My girl was happy my drought was over. *If only she knew.*

I opened my mouth and proceeded to tell Kayla the tale of the little engine that couldn't. I stopped the story to take a call and then continued. Kayla couldn't stop laughing. I laughed right along with her, but you best believe I was not laughing when it happened.

"What's really funny is that you killed my evening of romance to get some and didn't get any." She laughed. "Was it in?"

"Yes, it was in. Don't get me wrong, he has a nice size package, and I was able to sit on it, but as soon as I started moving, the ride came to an end."

We both laughed hysterically.

"Did he cum or it just turned soft?" Miss Nosy had to know everything.

"Kayla, personally I don't remember. All I know is I was not pleased."

"I can't believe you gave him a blowjob. You got played."

I rolled my eyes. "Thanks for reminding me."

"Well, did he at least slurp the smoothie?" she asked.

"Of course, Kayla, this is me. A prerequisite for sticking has always been licking. He sucked it. Slurped it. Licked it. All the tongue movements I like." The smile fell off of my face. "He just fell short in other ways."

"So you want me to go on air and tell the Tri-state area that Todd is not Mr. Luva Luva? That he is not the freak he claims to be? You want me to say he is large but damn sure not in charge?"

"He damn sure ain't in charge of keeping it up. A freak he might be." I grinned. "He did eat the hell out of the love palace. His tongue also visited another hole."

"Tae Tae, he tossed your salad?" Kayla cheesed.

I cheesed.

"Was he better than Curtis?" Kayla knew about Curtis and his tantalizing tongue.

"Oh, hell no!" I gave my girl a high five and rubbed the love below by holding my thighs tighter. Thinking of Curtis and his tongue gave a sistah flashbacks. "Nobody will ever compare to Curtis. I mean Jason is up there, but that damn Curtis just got pussy eating down to a damn science."

We laughed.

"I wish you had called me with this earlier. I would have gone on air with it this morning. But I'll use it tomorrow."

Kayla rose from her chair as I walked over to the closet to get my pink linen jacket. She turned the doorknob, opened the door, and then closed it. She knew how nosy Rosemary could be.

"Why do you want me to air this?"

"Just do it," I responded as I put on my jacket.

"Oh, I'm gonna do it." She cackled. "Todd might try to get funky or something. If so, I would like to know why I'd take that risk. By the way, I like that suit. What is that, Donna Karan?"

"Courtesy of my Daddy. You know he likes to buy me nice things." I smiled.

"Jason always had good taste," Kayla replied. "Now, why am I airing this?"

I knew Kayla was going to eventually ask that question. Actually, I thought the question would have been asked sooner. I answered her question by beginning with Jason calling me into his office that morning.

As we approached the elevators, I lowered my voice. I did not want Rosemary repeating anything I said during her gossip club lunch meetings.

"Is Jason jealous?" Kayla asked as soon as the elevator doors closed.

"I can't really tell. But you know he will always believe that my ass is his." I pressed the button for the 38th floor. "That's who called me when you first came into my office. He wants me to stop by his office before I leave."

Kayla knew good and well that our conversation was over as soon as we reached Jason's assistant, Doris' desk. Doris was the vice president of the gossip club. Jason's door was cracked, and Doris was nowhere in sight.

"What's so important that you needed to see me twice in one day?" I asked Jason with a smile as I walked into his office alone.

It was the incident all over again. In the middle of his office, Jason stood mouth fucking a familiar high yellow heifer. I wondered if this was why Jason had wanted me to come upstairs. Was it supposed to be me? Why would Jason expect me to give him head? I was high maintenance. I didn't give head for free; I received it and got paid for it.

"Uh um," I cleared my throat loudly. "Excuse me, Jason."

Jason immediately opened his eyes and attempted to pull his penis out of the whore's mouth. "Stop!"

Simone did not stop. It was like she wanted me to see her doing what she did best. Only the Lord kept me from grabbing her by her hair and slapping the shit out of her. If I were in a different state of mind, I would've gotten down on my knees and showed her the tricks of a real professional. I knew what Jason liked and all the spots that needed sucking, kissing, licking and caressing. However, I was not going to stoop down to the next bitch's level.

"Bitch, I said stop," " Jason yelled as he took his penis from her mouth. He pulled up his pants and proceeded to follow me. When he grabbed my arm, I snatched it away.

"Jason, let go of me," I said. After four years, this man still had an effect on me. I loved Jason with all my heart and he knew it. "Did you call me up here for this? Did you want me to see this?"

He held me tight and I embraced him. "No, I didn't call you to see this. I'm sorry you saw this. I'm also sorry you heard this bitch sucking me off over the phone. You know how I feel about you, but I got needs."

What the fuck does I have needs mean? I tried my best to analyze his statement, but that bitch was looking me in the eye and grinning. The Lord was still restraining me from knocking her out.

"You have needs? You have needs?" I grinned. "Well you know what, fucker, I have needs, too, and I need to receive those sandals on Kimora's feet." I pointed to the Baby Phat billboard outside of his window.

"Simone," Kayla yelled as she walked into the office. Her cousin was butt naked with a pair of gold sandals on, laying on the couch as if she were at a playboy photo shoot. "What in the hell are you doing?'

Kayla continued to curse Simone out. I wanted to thank Kayla for trying to defend me, but I did not need it. I was capable of taking care of myself. I no longer wanted to be in the presence of Jason and his whore. I walked out of his office with tears running down my face.

As I stood by the elevator, I heard Simone talking trash. I also heard Jason telling her to shut up.

I heard Kayla scream, "You're still sitting there butt naked after he called you a bitch? You think you got him? You ain't nothing but a mouth to him. Don't you know tomorrow Chante's going to have those sandals she just pointed out?

"You're fucking stupid! You think you did something 'cause your country ass fucked a celebrity. You think Jason's gonna make you famous? Jason don't give two shits about your country ass and I am sorry that I do."

The elevator was taking longer than it should have. The best thing about Jason's office was he didn't share the floor with anyone else. There was only his gigantic office and an assistant who sat outside his door. That was to my advantage because I did not want anyone to see me cry.

Funny thing was that when I first came upstairs, Doris was nowhere to be found. Yet, now she was at her desk staring me in my face, watching me cry.

"Mind your own fucking business," I yelled at her.

She gave me the 'no you didn't' look and continued to stare me down.

"Did you not comprehend what the hell I just said?"

I couldn't take it anymore. I needed to be alone. As soon as the elevator doors opened, I pressed L for lobby.

Six

"We don't have to go in if you don't want to." Kayla rubbed my shoulders as we sat outside of *With a Little Jazz Salon and Spa* in her BMW.

"Kayla, do you think my world stops because I caught some woman sucking Jason's dick? I'm not you. The world does not stop revolving around me just because a man cheats. I say fuck 'em. Kick his ass to the curb." I pretended that what I witnessed had no effect on me.

Kayla quickly removed her hand from my shoulder. I looked over to the left and noticed that my best friend had shifted her entire body away from me.

"I'm sorry, Kayla."

"You don't have to apologize." She removed her shades from the top of her head and placed them on her eyes.

I did have to apologize. I was wrong.

"Kayla, I had no right to bring your business to the table. I'm mad and I'm hurt because I saw your cousin sucking Jason off. I am not really bothered because it was your cousin. If it were any woman, I would feel the same. What hurts is that...never mind just forget it." I was about to reveal too much. I was about to confess my heart. My love for Jason was something that I kept to myself.

Just like a true diva, my game face was on when we walked into the day spa.

"Hello, ladies," I said accepting a champagne glass from Melanie, the receptionist.

"Do not walk up in here acting like you are bourgeois," Mecca, my beautician and friend, said as she sewed in a weave.

"Would you prefer I say what up bitches?" We laughed.

"Well, there are some bitches in here," Mecca replied rolling her eyes at the stylist in front of her.

"Chante, are you ready?" Sasha, the masseur asked.

"I want to start off with a mud bath," I said taking a bite out of my strawberry. "Tell Gina to get the Tranquility room ready. I don't want the raindrops and all that nature shit. Tell her to put on some Floetry or Maxwell. Better yet play anything from Mary J. Blige, preferably her Mary CD."

"Sasha, I'm ready," Kayla said handing her jean jacket and my linen jacket to Melanie to hang up.

"So what's the topic of the day?" I asked as Kim began to polish my nails.

"Whores." As Mecca touched up my highlights, she rolled her eyes at the stylist next to her.

Mecca and Faith, the other stylist, were always going at it. The only reason the two continued to work together was because *With a Little Jazz* was owned by Faith's half-sister, Tiffany, who was also Mecca's best friend.

"Fuck you, Mecca," Faith replied as she removed the curling iron from her client's hair and pointed it in Mecca's face.

This was my cue to get out of Mecca's chair. "Excuse me, Kim," I said getting up.

For the last six years, Mecca had been doing my hair. As a matter of fact, she used to do hair and makeup at Jason's World music division. I met her when she was the hair stylist for a show that I was producing. Jason fired her. The rumor was that Jason and Mecca became "close" and then she turned into a fatal attraction.

According to Mecca, she didn't sleep with Jason; she slept with his best friend, John, who currently ran the music video division. Mecca swore John was constantly harassing her for sex and a relationship. She said John was just a jump off. She had and still had a man at home. I didn't know if I believed Mecca or the rumor. If I had to bet money, I would bet on the rumor and replace Jason with John.

But anyway, we had been cool ever since. Mecca was one of my road dogs.

Kim backed up, and so did I. Kayla closed her magazine and got up out of Faith's chair.

"I've had enough drama today. Sean, finish my hair, please," Kayla said, plopping down in his brown leather chair.

Mecca and Faith constantly bumped heads, always over something stupid. It never failed. Mecca would make a comment. Faith would respond. Mecca would make another comment that followed up with a swing or the throwing of something.

With a Little Jazz was a classy, upscale, yet, ghetto salon, that held a lot of drama. If Mecca and Faith were not going at it, then Gina would be bragging about sleeping with someone else's man, or the guys from the barbershop next door were coming over to pick up chicks. I loved the place.

"Faith, I keep telling you I am not your goddamn child. I will kick your ass." Mecca motioned for me to sit back down.

I did.

"Bring it on, bitch." Faith must've forgotten whom she was talking to, or maybe she had eaten her Wheaties for breakfast.

"Bitch, it's brought." She damn near pushed me out of her chair.

"Damn." I laughed. "Look you two can fight later. I am a paying customer. Finish my hair."

"Oh, y'all look." Gina was staring out the huge window at a couple. "That's Kyle, but that woman he is kissing doesn't look jack like Michelle. Last night, Michelle was in here bragging about Kyle buying her a new car. They just bought a house. That heifer had the nerve to shake her hand in my face and tell me that asshole increased the diamond in her engagement ring."

Everyone was staring.

"I felt like saying Kyle must be slinging rock 'cause his broke ass ain't got no money. She was bragging about how he brought her a new car. What was it, a Honda? That nigga got bad credit, so I know he ain't buying no house. When we went to the hotel, I was pissed off I had to use my credit card because he didn't have one. I looked at her lying ass last night and was like can you leave now because we are about to close."

"You are so stupid, Mami," Sasha said, rolling her eyes. "That grown man has a credit card. He just couldn't use it to pay for a hotel room. How in the hell is he going to explain that to his wife? I keep telling you to leave those married men alone. One day one of their wives is going to cut ya ass."

Everyone laughed.

"And I am going to watch and laugh. Maybe even pass her the razor because that's what your slutty ass deserves," Sasha motioned for her next client.

"I know that's right." Kayla laughed giving Sasha a hi-five before she disappeared behind a brown swinging door.

Everyone laughed.

"Whatever!" Gina continued with her story.

It was gossip time now. All ears were glued to the conversation.

Me, I didn't want anything to do with the Kyle conversation. I went down his cheating lane before, and I would never go that route again. I met Kyle the same night Kayla met Shawn. We banged and it was great. The only thing I didn't find great was in the morning he wanted me to help him come up with a lie to tell his wife.

That should have been a stop sign for me. But instead I came up with a few more excuses to cover a short period of time. Call me stupid. I would. My only defense was that Kyle happened right after Jason and I had broke up. I was vulnerable. No one knew about Kyle, except me and him. And I wanted it to remain that way.

Seven

"Rosemary , who put this on my desk?" I asked standing in the doorway of my office.

"Jason went into your office with a Dior bag." She swiveled around in her chair toward me. "I have no idea who put that black envelope on your desk."

I found Rosemary had no clue how the envelope got on my desk odd; nothing seemed to get past her. I shrugged it off and went back into my office. I opened the envelope.

You are cordially invited to a Birthday Bash honoring
Mr. Keith Simmons
At
Uptowns
On
August 11, 2006.

I glanced over at my desk calendar; the eleventh was today. I had no idea who Keith Simmons was, but if he wanted me at his birthday party, I would be a good girl and attend.

Now let's hope and pray I could get Mecca to fit me in.

Courtesy of my daddy, I did not have to go out and buy a new outfit. Instead I had to choose between all the new things he bought me. I was definitely wearing my constellation prize for witnessing Simone giving head. My sandals were waiting on my desk for me the next day after witnessing that catastrophe. Jason wanted to make sure his Tae Tae was satisfied. The days following, I received more shopping bags.

Would it be the black Badgley Mischka LBD with the plunging neckline? Or would a sistah choose the red Vera Wang? How about I spice it up with a little color and wear the orange floral print Robert Cavalli. Back and forth I walked from my dressing room to my bedroom. I took things out of the closet and laid them on the bed. I picked them up from the bed and took them back into the closet. I settled on the black Marc Jacobs ruffled dress my daddy had delivered to me today. The dress was short and sexy.

"Hello," I answered the phone on the first ring.

"Hi, Ms. Chambers." It was Franklin. "Your car is here."

"I'll be right down."

"Would you get your ass in the limo and stop trying to be cute? It ain't no paparazzi out here," Mecca said, referring to the fact that I was standing outside the limo shaking my head full of loose curls.

In my head I was one of those ladies in the movies that stood still while her hair blew in the wind, and all the men admired her. To my dismay, there wasn't a soul outside except Franklin and the limo driver who was patiently waiting for me to get in the car.

"We see you." Mecca frowned. "Now will you please get in the damn limo? It's hot out there and you are letting out all the cold air from the AC."

I rolled my eyes at Mecca as the door closed behind me. I didn't know how I allowed Mecca to invite herself to the party. Yes, I did, it was either let her come or she wasn't going to do my hair.

"Mecca, you look cute." I sipped some champagne.

"It's Versace." She smiled. "You like?"

I liked the jacket with no shirt or bra underneath and matching booty shorts up until she told me the designer's name. I had nothing against Versace, but was it really that important for me to know who the designer was? I thought not.

"Is that platinum?" Mecca asked, pointing to my chandelier earrings, necklace and bracelet that my daddy bought me.

One thing I hated about Mecca was that everything had to be a name brand and the next person had to know which brand it was. Everything in my closet had an expensive price tag attached to it, but it wasn't in my nature to brag about it.

"It's Dior." I turned my back to her and looked out the window. "You figure it out."

♫

"Gold Digger" by Kanye West was blasting through the speakers at Uptowns. I loved this song. I was doing the over the shoulder thing that Kanye does in the video while I sang along with the chorus. The deejay switched up the pace. He played some music from the dirty south. Rick Ross' "Hustling" was now playing. This was my song. *Hustling. Hustling. Hustling. Everyday I'm hustling. Everyday I'm hustling.*

My breast bounced up and down, and my dress kept sliding off my shoulder as I popped my thang to the music. "You know it had to be a remix, right?" I laughed. The woman that sat next to me in the VIP room looked at me. "I said you know it had to be a remix, right?" She said, "Um hum." Maybe she thought that would shut me up but little did she know she hadn't heard anything yet. "Who the fuck you think you fucking with, I'm the fucking boss. Five foot seven, bubbling brown bombshell. A bitch who loves to floss..." I bopped my head and continued to bop to the music making up my own rhymes.

As the music thumped, my head was thumping more. I walked over to the balcony that overlooked the club. I somewhat regretted telling the barmaid to keep the mango mai tais coming to my table. I searched the crowd for Mecca. Knowing her the way I did, she was wherever the ballers were.

As soon as we arrived at Uptowns she went her way, I went mine, straight to the bar. I started the night with two glasses of champagne in the limo. About an hour after arriving at the club, I had the bartender refill my frozen sangria. After that I worked my way over to a strawberry daiquiri. A handsome bald gentleman bought me a margarita, and I thought a woman bought the martini. It didn't matter who bought what, I drank it all.

I was drunk beyond my normal level of drunkenness. A sistah was still cute though. I was slightly stressing over that shit with Jason, not to mention horny. Before I knew it I had lost my grip on the balcony's railing and was falling backwards. Before my Marc Jacobs covered butt touched the floor, a very handsome caramel-colored Adonis broke my fall. I blinked twice just to make sure I wasn't dreaming.

He winked, and I looked into his light brown eyes. I could not believe he was staring back at me with those sexy dreamy, droopy bedroom eyes. You know the eyes Busta Rhymes had in that video with Mariah Carey? Yeah, those come fuck me eyes. I smiled as I admired him from head to toe while he helped me up.

Mr. Caramel was polished, very polished in a pretty boy way. His black shoes were shining. His butt was calling me from the inside of his pants to grab it. His white button down shirt clung to his muscles as his tie lay undone around his shoulders. I noticed his frostbitten wrist when he grabbed me by the waist. I was intoxicated on more than just the liquor. He smiled back at me as I smiled at him.

"It looks like you've had too much to drink." He helped me get it together and took a seat next to me on the blue velvet couch.

"I wouldn't say that." Here I was trying to be cute and I'd almost fell of the couch. Once again Mr. Carmel was there to break my fall. He instructed the barmaid to bring us two bottles of water.

"Do you want to go get some air?"

I would have gone anywhere he asked me to go.

"This is my song." I started dancing my way toward the door. We never made it outside. The deejay just kept playing my jams. And I kept Mr. Carmel dancing. I rubbed my butt all over his crotch and felt his nature rising and rising. I was shaking my money maker for Ludacris and Pharrell.

Once the deejay switched to club music, my stilettos were glued to the dance floor. I started dipping on him just to see if he could work with it and he did. Mr. Caramel kept right up with me.

As a treat, I combined all the booty shaking dance routines I picked up from music videos and started shaking my thing because I was still in love with this song. My butt fit into Mr. Caramel's crotch like a puzzle piece. The only thing in between Mr. Caramel and me hitting it doggie style was Marc Jacobs.

The music switched from club back to hip-hop. We were leaning and rocking with it with Dem Franchise Boys when all of a sudden I noticed the spotlight was on us. In my head I heard Tupac's "All Eyez On Me."

"I like to send a birthday shout out to the birthday man, none other than the pretty boy himself, Founder and CEO of *Pretty Boy Records*, Mr. Keith Simmons." The Deejay's voice rang throughout the club.

Everyone started clapping as I stood embarrassed. I had no clue whom I was dancing with.

"Happy Birthday, Keith." I tried to excuse myself.

"Wait, Chante, don't go." He held onto my arm. "You can't leave without having a piece of cake." He smiled.

Oh my God! He just licked his lips like LL COOL J. I didn't know any woman who could resist LL licking his lips. This man was sexy. As I came down from my high, I wondered how he knew who I was.

"Um, Keith…"

He must have been reading my mind. "Chante, you are a very beautiful woman. I saw you in *Essence Magazine*, and I knew I had to meet you. How do you think you got the invite to the party?"

Keith smiled as I wondered how my hands would feel twirling through the curls on his head. I was a sucker for men with baldheads, waves, or even the curly stuff. I didn't mean that s-curl stuff. I meant the natural stuff. Keith had the natural stuff.

I had forgotten all about the damn invitation and being invited to a party. All I remembered was getting dolled up to get my party on.

The rest of the night was a blur in the morning. When I woke up Keith was lying beside me. We never made it into the bedroom. Nor did we sleep together. Well, we did, but not in that way. I was lying on the white sofa with a blanket over me and Keith was asleep on the loveseat.

He was even handsome in his sleep. He looked so peaceful. I saw why his record company was called *Pretty Boy Records*. Damn, my breath stunk. Keith could not wake up and see me like this, at least not right now. I rushed into the bathroom and took off my clothes and jumped in the shower. I was happy that he hadn't tried to take advantage of me. My panties were still on as proof.

There was something about my shower that made me horny every time I entered it. I was tempted to play T-Boz again and touch myself. Yet, there was no way in hell I was going to rub my clitoris or allow the shower water to fall over it at full speed when I had an Adonis the size of a football player in my living room. *Should I? Shouldn't I?* I didn't know Keith well enough to give him a piece of me. I didn't know him at all. However, I did have some *magnums* in my drawer on reserve, just in case.

I shook the thought of screwing a stranger out of my head. Instead, I closed my eyes and envisioned that stranger in the shower with me. Keith kissed my lips. He worked his way down my ears and my neck. I opened my mouth and gasped as he played with my spots. His hands cupped my breast, and I melted. His fingertips explored every crack and crevice of my body until it found my warmth. Each circle his fingertip made around my love button produced a different movement, a different sound, a different expression. I was satisfied. I washed my ass and got out of the shower.

I didn't have to sleep with Keith just yet. I didn't want him to think I was easy or that I was a hoe. In the meantime I could fantasize about him. So instead of putting on my black silk robe with the matching lace boy cut briefs, I opted for my white hooded terry cloth robe and headed for the kitchen. I knew I should have put on some panties, but I was prepared for the unexpected.

As I scrambled the eggs, I felt warm kisses on my neck. Keith held my hair up and kissed the back of my neck. A chill went through me. He must have chewed a piece of gum because I could taste the spearmint on his tongue as he moved it around in my mouth. He picked me up, and sat me on the island. His tongue never left my mouth, yet his hands explored every part of my body.

I wanted to stop Keith. I wanted to warn him, that if he came in two minutes he would be subjected to being killed. Instead, I enjoyed his tongue as it ran over my nipples. My neck rolled back as Keith french kissed my nipples. If I went through with this, what would he think of me? Would he still respect me? I decided to clear my mind and just take this for what it was, sex.

Oh my God! The size of Keith's johnson had a sistah dazed for a moment. My cat began to purr when Keith exposed himself to her. I opened my legs a little wider and he slid himself in. Keith was gentle and slow. Each stroke possessed more passion than the one before. He worked me until I could not work anymore. He was definitely not a Todd.

We were working it out on my kitchen counter. I wrapped my legs around him, dug my fingernails into his back, and instructed him to lie down on the floor. I couldn't take much more of it. I was ready to collapse; he took his sweet time to reach his peak. Hell, I was working on my fourth explosion.

Next thing I knew we were both smoking cigarettes on my kitchen floor. The bacon was burnt and my smoke detector was going off. Nothing mattered at that moment. I had finally gotten what I had wanted for so long. And it was good! *THANK YOU, LORD!*

"Do you want to go out for breakfast?" Keith asked.

Keith was the man. Mr. Caramel had me smoking a cigarette and I did not smoke. As we lay on the kitchen floor, I felt my heart beating faster. I thought it was going to burst out of my chest. My adrenaline was up on high. I had to take a couple of deep breaths before I spoke.

Inhale.

Exhale.

Inhale.

Exhale.

"Aren't you going to change your clothes?" I rolled over into Keith's arms. True he had given me great sex, but he was not going anywhere with me in yesterday's sweaty clothes.

"If you want, we can go into the city. I can shower, change my clothes, and have my housekeeper cook us up something. Or we can hit a mall, get me an outfit and eat here in Jersey." He extended his hand to pull me up off the tiled floor.

"How about we take a shower, then we can come back into the kitchen and try to make breakfast again?" I grinned as Keith helped me up.

I gave him a towel and led him to the master bathroom. At that moment, I knew Keith was mine until I didn't want him anymore. I have had one-nightstands before, and none of them had ever stayed for breakfast. Keith was different. I was going to like Mr. Simmons.

"Chante, aren't you coming?" Keith summoned me into bathroom. I followed.

Eight

I laid sprawled out across my bed in the nude singing, "I Want to Fuck You." I sang the explicit version of Akon and Snoop Dog's song while the radio played the clean version. This song should have been on while Keith helped me get through my drought.

Kayla's show, *Waking up to Gossip on Blazing 99*, was blasting from my clock radio. I could not descend from the rapture I had got caught up in. My head was killing me from banging it into the headboard over and over; Keith knew his thrust was nothing to mess with. I was swimming in wetness. Keith had eaten me for breakfast, and I hadn't moved. I had been in the same spot for the last two hours, with a smile plastered across my face.

Only Keith knew if his intentions were to lie around all day and get me whooped. He had done a hell of a job doing so. The brother had me missing work Thursday and Friday. Working at home my ass, I was working on that Kama Sutra book and Keith, that's what I was doing. As much as I wanted to "work at home" again today, I had a television pilot to sell to a network. I kissed big Keith and little Keith goodbye.

"For everybody just waking up to gossip with Kayla," Kayla voice piped through the radio, "get ya butts up! It's gossip time!"

Sometimes, Kayla got on my nerves with her gossip. She talked about everybody and anybody. If you had a name and some dirt in your book bag, Kayla told it all. I had forewarned her about spilling anything that went on at Jason's World that involved me. Kayla and I had been friends since the first grade, and she said she would never jeopardize our friendship.

"...And there's a little rumor going on in the maternity ward that super model Layla Michaels is expecting a baby by none other than the very married football player Jonathan McGee. A reliable source at the courthouse has informed me that his wife has filed for divorce..."

All of the men in the McGee family were dogs. Jason's cousin Jonathan had been married for only a year and was having a baby with another woman.

"Now let's dish the dirt on the other McGee. You know Jason, music video extraordinaire, TV and movie producer. The P-Diddy of the film industry..."

I had to laugh at that. In Jason's eyes, he was much bigger than Puff Daddy.

"Well, ladies, it looks like there's trouble in Jason's World..."

If Kayla said it, I was going to call up to that station and curse her out on the air. Was she going to go there?

"As I hear it, Jason has women fighting over him. That's right, insiders report that his ex whooped a bitch's ass. I know all of you are like which ex. I'll keep you guessing at that one. I'll give you one clue; she's the *one* that matters. But anyway as I hear it, after someone got caught with their pants around their ankles while another party was on her knees," a sucking and smacking sound was played, "The boxing gloves were on. I guess that knob slobber had no idea who she was messing with. Doesn't she know this ex ain't the bitch to be f-ed with?" Kayla giggled. "Some say the fight started because the knob slobber..." The sound effect was played again. "was upset because Jason didn't do her. Others say she was jealous."

A snippet of the classic "Put It in Your Mouth" was playing in the background. Kayla sang along with the song for a brief moment.

"Jason, is it really that good that you have women fighting over you?" Kayla asked. "The whole situation sounds very pathetic to me. What do you think, New York? Let's take it to the phones. Speaking of pathetic, I am still taking calls from anyone who's had the displeasure of being with Todd. Call me up...."

Before Kayla was finished giving out the radio stations phone number, I was waiting on hold to speak with the gossip princess.

"I'm being told I have a hater on line one," Kayla said. "I hope it's the King of Jason's World. What's your name and where are you calling from?"

"This is the Queen of Jason's World," a woman said, "and I am calling from the empire."

Now who the hell was this B on the radio? I was still on hold.

"Oh, well I'm the Gossip Princess. If you got some dirty

laundry, I'm sure as hell going to air it. So what's you beef?" Kayla never missed a beat. One thing about Kayla, she only told the truth.

"I don't know where you get off ruining people's lives. Jason is my man, and he ain't jealous of nobody. Nor is he pathetic. If anything his ex is jealous of me because I got everything she wants."

"First of all, Ma Ma, how's the eye? Secondly, I heard you were the one who was jealous since Jason stopped you from doing what you do best after you two were interrupted. Third, you know you don't compare to the ex, you said the wrong thing and got ya ass whooped." She took a breath. "Look here, little Miss Jason...if Jason is your man and you're sitting on the throne next to him, why don't you put him on the phone, so we can hear the story straight from the dog's mouth. Please don't start crying, Little Miss Jason, because you will shed a tear after finding out you're only in the picture because the one who is really wanted doesn't want Jason. You are a substitute." Kayla laughed.

I hung up the phone and turned off the radio. Who in the world told Kayla that I had to rough Simone up? I purposely lied when I told Kayla I left my wallet on my desk. I made sure she went to go get her SUV from the parking garage before I took my steaming mad ass back into the building and up to the 38th floor. And it wasn't an actual fight; the only thing I did was punch Simone in the face, once or twice.

I would handle Kayla another time. I had walked into Jason's office alone. Despite what I saw when I entered Jason's office, I had not called Kayla into the office, nor did I discuss my feelings with her afterwards. I purposely did not make a scene because I didn't want any of my actions to be heard on the air.

I knew Kayla would defend me to the so-called *empresses* of Jason's World. I also knew that Jason was reacting the same way as I had. I made a mental note to make a trip to the 38th floor to tell Jason to set his boo straight. There would be no drama in Big Mama's domain. I was and would always be the Queen of Jason's World, whether I was screwing him or not.

"Chante, these are for you," Rosemary handed me a beautiful bouquet of white roses.

"Either you rocked his world, or Kayla is sorry." Rosemary was too damn nosy for her own good. "I heard the show. I thought she was your girl." Rosemary was once again minding my business. I made a mental note that she could no longer play the radio at her desk.

I just smiled. "No, I just rocked his world." It was the truth. I did rock his world, just not the him she was referring to.

I sat at my desk admiring the card. It read:

I had a lovely long weekend.
I would love to see you again tonight.
Love, Keith

The smile on my face vanished when Jason arrived. His smile surprised me. I guess my rumor made its way to the 38th floor since Jason was standing before me with a smile wide as day. Rosemary moved faster than the speed of light.

"What did I do now to get a visit from the King?" I pretended to be looking over some papers.

"Did you finalize the script to *The Other Woman*?" He sat down without being invited.

"Um hum."

"Is everything alright with *On the Block*?"

"Um hum."

"Who sent you flowers?" He made himself comfortable.

"Why don't you guess?" I wrote something down on my notepad.

"Well, I know they're not from Todd since he doesn't wanna work with you. Which can mean either one of two things, either you teased my man and wouldn't give up the butt or you gave him some wack ass pussy." He shifted his balls and winked.

"You didn't give up no wack pussy. I don't even think that's possible. Ain't shit wack about your love palace, right? You still it call it that? The love palace? You know how to tease a nigga though."

He made sure to reposition his balls while I was looking at his crotch. Jason made me sick. What's more sickening was that he was turning me on.

"We both know the love palace is hot," I said it the way Paris Hilton says 'that's hot.' "If you must know, I spoon-fed him this good ass pussy, and the brother couldn't hang."

Jason laughed. "Oh my God. That cat was quick." He laughed again. "I volunteered to bang your back out, and you turned me down that night."

"Well, I'm pretty sure that did not stop you from banging someone else's back out. Now did it?" I was still mad at him. "Jason, what did you come here for?"

"Because when I see a beautiful woman I like to stare at her." He laughed. He was referring to Todd's explanation of our kiss at the movie premiere. He could tell I was pissed and annoyed by him, so he got to the point.

"I love you, Tae Tae."

"Oh, so now I'm Tae Tae? Last week I was Chante." I stopped writing to get a real good look at him. I wanted to see if he was sincere or not.

"Look, I know you heard what Simone said on the radio."

"Oh, so the fact that I caught her sucking your dick wasn't enough? So she's the queen in Jason's little world? So, uh…ya girl thinks I'm jealous?" I tested Jason by sitting on top of the desk in front of him in a short jean skirt. I purposely pulled up my skirt to sit and crossed my legs and revealed my bare butt.

"What am I jealous of, Jason?" I allowed him to speak, but made it my business to shift my legs. To top it off, I undid another button on my red shirt. "Is it hot in here or is it me?"

My cleavage was just the way I wanted it, all in Jason's face. My nipples said hello to him.

"Why you mad? She was the one with the black eye." He laughed. "Tae Tae, you attacked her."

"Are you looking for me to apologize to her or something?"

"Look, Tae Tae, don't start. I didn't even come down here for all of that. I can admit I was jealous over Todd. I can't see why you wanted that dude over me. Believe me when I say I did not call you up to my office to see that. I called you like a half hour before you came. I actually thought you weren't coming. You know how you are.

"But I came down here to say I was sorry bout the shit in my office and I'm sorry about what you heard on the radio. I did not authorize any of that shit." His eyes stayed glued to my tits and my thighs.

Whatever, Jason!

"Okay, your apology was accepted when I received the Versace, Neiman Marcus, Marc Jacobs and Dior shopping bags and we can't forget the Prada collection."

"I'm serious, Chante."

"Jason, what did you really come downstairs for?"

Jason came downstairs to have sex because his head was now in between my thighs. Prior to Thursday I couldn't fall on some dick, now everyone wanted to taste me.

My brain was sending messages to my mouth to stop him. However, my thighs would not unlock from around his head. All I could do was push his head in deeper and rolled my neck back.

I thought about Keith. I thought about Thursday morning in the kitchen, our afternoon in the shower, and our evening on top of the piano. Hell, I thought about all day Friday and how it was spent in my bed, just cuddling. I should have had enough, but I couldn't say no to Jason hitting it doggie style. I screamed, "Fuck me, Daddy" every time he smacked my backside.

It was not in my plans to break in my new mahogany desk with Jason, but there I was bent over it. I hoped and prayed Rosemary did not walk in.

"Oh Daddy," I moaned, as Jason showed me all that I had been missing.

"Who's ya daddy?" Smack.

"You are. I love Daddy's dick."

He pulled my hair, which turned me on more. I turned my head to face him, just so he could see the pleasure he brought me via my facial expressions. He kissed me.

"I love you, girl. Tell me you miss Daddy's dick." Smack.

"I missed Daddy's Dick."

I guess I got too loud because Jason removed his free hand from my breast and placed it over my mouth.

I felt great after Jason penetrated my insides. Jason was cleaning his juices off of the print throw rug when I came out of my personal bathroom. He smiled and watched me as I buttoned my shirt and put on my red thong. I pulled my skirt down and readjusted my belt. I sat down in my chair and stared at Jason with a straight face.

"What?" He grinned.

"Although my stuff is great, I know you didn't come down here for that. So what did you really come down here for?"

Jason had a motive behind everything he did. I knew the sex thing had not been planned; like many men he had no ability to resist my strong brown thighs. I did not know whether his apology was sincere or not.

"I have somebody for the role of Maya." I knew it. That S.O.B. slept with some chick and wanted to make her famous. I was disgusted. I just had sex with this could be STD-infected motherfucker without any protection and all along he wanted me to put one of his hoes on.

I wanted to snap. I wanted to knock his head into my computer. Before I blew up, I contemplated whether or not his homicide could be justified. Quickly I scanned my desk for the best murder weapon. Jason f-ed me for one of his bimbos. *DUMB! I was so damn DUMB!*

"Now you're paying me off with sex? What happened to you bribing me with Birken bags? Don't tell me Prada's getting too expensive for you? Was it the wardrobe you bought? Giuseppe's costing too much for you these days? So now you have to resort to giving sexual favors?" I stood and walked over to the door. "You know damn well auditions were held last week. You also knew I had a few people in mind and were bringing them in for callbacks tomorrow. Don't come in here telling me you have someone for the part of my leading actress."

"Nah, Tae Tae, it ain't even like that. Won't you stop thinking that I'm out to hurt you or use you?" I was holding the doorknob to let him out. "Look, Chante. I'm tired of being without you. I want you in my life as my lady and what we just did was not a pay off. Shit, I miss you and I miss that." He pointed to my love palace.

"If you miss me and love me so much, why do you sleep with all those other girls?"

"'Cause you ain't my girl. Remember you don't want to be her. So I gotta fuck somebody in the meantime. I got needs." Jason always thought that was a good excuse.

"I take it you just happened to fuck Simone?"

"Here you go. Look, I met Simone at the premiere. You wasn't trying to catch it. We exchanged numbers. She met me at a club, got on her knees and sucked my dick. That day in my office, that just happened. I keep telling you that. She ain't nothing but a hoe."

"She ain't nothing but my best friend's cousin." I couldn't stand Simone. Right now I was really hating, yet she was still my best friend's cousin.

"Oh shit!" He thought for a minute. "Simone is Kayla's cousin? Chante, I swear I didn't know that. If I knew I would not have messed with her."

"But you slept with her! She's calling radio stations claiming to be your queen. The chick was sucking you off and looking at me as if to throw it in my face. Jason, save your bullshit for the next one because I don't have the time or the patience for you to break my heart again." I opened the door. "And one more thing, let that bitch know that I'm the queen of this motherfucker!"

"Well since you feel that way," Jason reached into his pocket, "let's call us even." He pulled a stack of crispy one hundred dollar bills from his wallet and placed it on my desk and left.

Nine

Miki Howard's beautiful voice drifted through my bathroom. Once again I was feeling like shit. My neighbors had to be tired of listening to "Love under New Management." Hell, I was. Prior to that, I had been listening to Meshell Ndegeocello's "Fool of Me." A fool was exactly what I felt like. Every time the song stopped, I played it again. The first verse kept calling my attention. After a while, I stopped playing the entire song all the way through. The first verse would begin, and I would sing along. As soon as the first chorus ended, I pressed replay to start the song over again.

Miki was singing to me. There was a lesson to be learned in this song. I didn't know who the hell wrote the song, and I was not about to take the time to read the CD cover to find out; however, I swear the song was written with me in mind.

As I soaked in the tub, I stared into the flames of the pink passion scented candles that adorned the tub. I grasped everything Ms. Howard was singing. I cried as I sang the chorus. Once again I was in concert. I stood in the tub, left arm extended; the back scratcher/microphone was to my right. I sang my heart out.

That son of a bitch! He considered us even with only a few thousand dollars. Now Jason knew the palace was worth more than a couple thousand dollars. A car arrived after our last sexcapade. It hurt my feelings more than I wanted to admit. And to think that was the man I loved. The man that I would steal for and kill for just paid for me like I was some damn prostitute or something. When would I learn that Jason couldn't be trusted?

As the tears continued to fall, I sang along with Phil Perry singing "Love Don't Love Nobody." I felt stupid. I felt dirty. I felt dumber than a dumb ass. I wanted to call Keith and cancel our dinner plans. That morning, Keith had made me feel good in so many ways. That man had made me breakfast, served it to me in bed, and then ate me for breakfast. All day Sunday, Keith's goal was to get to know me. He wanted to know all about me, my childhood, my likes, dislikes, wants, hopes, and dreams.

No one had taken an interest in me like that in God knows how long. How could I have disappointed the only man that made me smile in a very long time? Jason was the man I loved. Yet, treated me like a whore. I would not allow him to ruin my one chance at happiness. There was no time to feel sorry for myself. I had slept with the dirty dog knowing he did not have good intentions. I just had to deal with the humiliation. From here on out, Chante Chambers was in love under new management.

"Chante? Chante?" I heard Keith calling.

"I'm in the bathroom," I shouted.

Keith walked into the bathroom. All I could do was smile. I was impressed. I left the front door open and advised the doorman to let Keith up as soon as he arrived.

"Do you still want to go out to dinner?" he asked.

"Yes. What time is it?"

"It's 7:20," Keith replied looking at his ice-covered Rolex. "We have reservations at Cha la Keith's at 8:15." He smiled.

"Cha la Keith's? Is that a new restaurant?"

"It's my kitchen." He laughed.

I knew the answer to the question. I just wanted to see those dimples.

"Well, I can move faster if you help me." A smirk graced my face.

Keith stood back and evaluated the situation. He removed a pink towel from the towel rack and laid it on the floor. He got down on his knees. Stuck his hand in my bubble bath and grabbed my loofah. He lathered it up and proceeded to wash me.

♫

As we pulled up in front of Keith's Upper Westside penthouse, I kept staring at him. I could really learn to love this man. In my head I sung "I Love Me Some Him" by Toni Braxton. It had been over thirty minutes since Keith lathered me up and I was still tingling on the inside and outside. Sistah girl was glowing!

Across the street from Keith's penthouse was Central Park. The moon could not be found across the Hudson River in Jersey, but it was shining bright over a couple sitting in a parked Maserati. It was the perfect background for the perfect date.

"What are you thinking about?" he asked.

"Would you mind walking through the park with me before we go inside?"

Keith laughed.

"What's so funny?"

"I never had anyone ask me that before." He placed his car in park and took his foot off the brakes.

"Good evening, Miss Chambers," the doorman said as he opened the passenger door of Keith's sedan.

I smiled. "Hello."

"Are you in for the night, Mr. Simmons?" he asked as Keith stepped away from the car.

"I don't know. It's up to the lady." Keith looked at me and grinned.

"How did the doorman know my name?"

His dimples were highly visible. "I prepared for our date tonight," Keith answered. He grabbed my hand, and we crossed the street.

It was the middle of August, and all week long the weather had been hot and humid. Tonight it was chilly. The wind blew my hair all over the place. As we began to walk I regretted asking Keith to walk with me in the park. My three-inch heels were killing me. With every step, the sandals felt like torture, but they looked good with my white cropped pants and a white halter top. My shoulders were freezing, yet I tried my best to act like I was not cold.

Keith took off his jacket and placed it around my shoulders. As we walked in silence, I held Keith's arm while my head rested on his shoulder.

He shocked me by actually agreeing to walk with me. I dated enough celebrities to know they had problems with doing stuff like this. I was looking too cute to get robbed, and I damn sure couldn't run in these heels. If I did I would look like the white girl that always fell down in a scary movie. Occasionally, I glanced over my shoulder to make sure no one was following us.

"Thank you," I said breaking the silence.

"What are you thanking me for?" he asked.

"For doing something that I like."

"So you like walking through the park in stilettos?" Keith joked.

"I like to do a lot of things in stilettos," I replied in a sexy tone.

Keith gave me a sexy grin.

"No, Mr. Jokester." I laughed. "I remembered I was wearing three inch heels after we began walking. But really, I enjoy taking walks. It's hard to find someone of your stature who is willing to do little things like this."

"So, are you looking for someone to do little things like this with?"

It was funny that although Keith and I had slept together more than once, and had spent the entire weekend at my condo ordering in, this was our first date.

"To be honest, no. But it looks like I found someone who I could consider doing little things like this with for a while." I smiled.

"Oh, really."

"Yes, really." We stopped walking and I stood in front of Keith. "Keith, I want you to know that what happened back at my house on Thursday and the rest of the weekend, I don't normally do things like that."

Keith looked at me like he did not have a clue what I was talking about.

"I don't bring men home from clubs and have sex with them. I am not that type of girl."

"Chante, I know who I left Uptowns with and that was not a slut." He looked down into my eyes.

Why did Keith have to mention the word slut? Why did he have to look me directly in the eyes? I was a slut. I felt like he was reading me and he knew my secret. I had sex with him that morning and had sex with Jason in the afternoon. Now, here I was on a date with him. If I wasn't a slut when he came home with me, I was damn sure a slut now.

"I don't want you to think that I leave clubs with women with ideas of sexing them. What I saw at *Uptowns* was a beautiful woman, whom I was waiting all night to meet. I didn't expect our meeting to involve me picking you up off the floor, or off the curb, but hey, I still thought you were sexy drunk and all."

We both laughed.

I remembered falling off the railing onto the floor, and almost falling off the couch. I had no recollection of falling outside. "I fell outside?"

"Yes, you did." Keith laughed. "I don't know what you had to drink, but you were fucked up."

"Yes, I was. I had the hangover to prove it." We began walking again. "You did not help my hangover either."

"I was trying to get your mind on something else." He smirked. "Look, I know your feet hurt, and you had goose bumps on your shoulder, so would you like to go eat now?"

"Yes, I would."

"Keith, dinner was delicious." I sipped my glass of champagne.

"Can the cook have a kiss?" Keith's dimples screamed for me to jump all over them.

I felt like giving him more than just a kiss. I wanted to unzip my pants, take them off, pull my thongs over to the side, pull Keith's chair back, unzip his zipper, pull Lil Keith out and jump on it. But I couldn't because I was a lady. I liked Keith. He and I were finished eating in less than an hour after we started, yet three hours later we were still sitting at his dining room table talking and drinking champagne. The candles that once stood tall had practically burned down, but the flames were still flickering.

I pulled my chair away from the table, and with my most seductive 'you are America's Next Top Model' walk, I approached Keith. I bent down and pushed my tongue inside his mouth. Feeling the warmth of his mouth made me want to share the warmth of my body with him. Keith kissed me back with the same passion. I wasn't sure if he wanted me in the same manner that I wanted him. I wanted to push all the dishes off of the cherry wood table and onto the floor and let this man make sweet love to me on his dining room table.

Keith had other plans for me. He pulled back his chair, held my hand and gave me a tour of his penthouse. Outside on the terrace, Keith showed me the stars and the moon.

Ten

As I dressed, Keith sat patiently on the chaise in my bedroom. Our date was supposed to start at four, or at least that's the time I was told to be ready. It was a quarter to five, and I was standing in my dressing room in a black lace bra, matching boy cut briefs, a pair of black thigh highs and a pair of funky black Manolo Blahniks. As I put on my diamond earrings, a gift from my new daddy, I noticed Keith leaning against the frame of the doorway.

I wondered how long he had been standing there. It was over thirty minutes ago that I left him in my bedroom. Over the past eight weeks, I noticed Keith watched me a lot. His handsome face always had a sexy grin on it, just like it did now.

"How long have you been standing there?" I asked. I hope he hadn't seen me trying to shake my booty like Beyoncé.

"Long enough to have seen your Beyoncé routine."

I laughed. I could have been ready forty-five minutes ago, but instead I was watching *106 and Park* on BET. I was glad my decorator talked me into installing a flat screen TV in my dressing room. I reasoned that I could check the weather before I dressed. But lately the weather was not what I was checking out.

"How much longer do you think you are going to be?" he asked still leaning against the wall.

"I'm sorry about having you wait. Give me another twenty minutes. I just have to put my clothes on," I said, taking my soft pink blouse off the hanger. "Keith, can you fasten this for me?" I held my hair up as he fastened the clasp of my necklace.

Gently he kissed the back of my neck. "You're welcome."

Keith's kiss raised the hairs on the back of my neck. Chills ran through my body as my nipples showed they were alive. If Keith did that again, I would need more than twenty minutes. I would need at least twenty-five to thirty minutes to change my wet panties.

Keith's touch had my body programmed. The first kiss caused my nipples to harden. The kiss he just planted on my lips made my love palace tingle. As his tongue touched my neck, my pink and black pinstriped pants fell out of my hands and onto the floor. I couldn't go a day without craving that man. Keith had me sprung, not just sexually. He took a sistah to another level with each encounter.

Keith's hand rested on my waist as my arms were around his neck. His johnson pressed against my love palace, which caused a thunderstorm.

"Can I have some love right now?" I asked as I began to unbutton his shirt.

Damn, was all I could say when I buried my head in his muscular chest. I loved looking at him in his wife beater undershirt.

"How much love do you want?" He bent down and lifted my chin and kissed me gently on the lips. "Is that enough?"

"No, baby, that is not enough." I gazed into his light brown eyes.

"How about this?" He pushed his tongue through my lips and french kissed me like the world was about to end.

"That's a start." I gasped for air.

"We don't have time for much of anything else. I keep telling you my surprise can't wait. I want you to meet an important lady in my life." Keith talked as I unfastened his belt. He didn't stop me from unzipping his pants either.

Keith was really making a big deal out of my meeting his mother. The plan was for us to go out to dinner and to a play. I was sorry, but Mama would have to understand if we were a little late. I had needs that Keith was going to fulfill.

"Do we have time for this?" I kneeled down and proceeded to suck him.

Keith did not ask me to get up. He did not say stop. Time stopped being important when the moisture from my mouth touched his friend. Keith did not fight the pleasure. Instead he grabbed a handful of my hair and stared me in the eyes as I took all of him in.

He pulled me up after he released and wiped my mouth. He instructed me to bend over the dresser in the middle of my dressing room. I was a good soldier and always did as instructed. I was ready to be entered from behind. I waited patiently to feel him inside, and when I didn't, I turned around to find Keith admiring me. He kissed my lips, neck and nibbled on my ears. He worked his way down to my breasts. He sucked, licked, nibbled and bit until a sistah was screaming his name.

"Keith, Keith!" I was about to cum.

"You wanted it. Now take it," he ordered.

"Make me take it," I screamed.

My head rolled back as Keith kissed and caressed my breast, his pointer and middle finger caressed, pulled and played with my spot until my juices were all over his hand. Keith knew my spots, and he was aiming for all of them. I closed my eyes as he licked my belly button and kissed the inside of my thighs. My body shook.

I opened my eyes after Keith stopped touching me.

"Are you okay now?" Keith grinned. "Are you satisfied?"

"Boy, you better stop playing," I yelled.

"You want it? Beg for it," Keith commanded

"Keith, please come fuck me," I whined.

He stared at me with a blank face.

"I'm sorry. Keith, Baby, please come make love to me?" I bent over the dresser. "Please, Baby?"

Keith's dimples said hello to me as he entered me from behind.

"You like that?" he asked.

I did not respond.

"Answer me!" Keith really liked this role-playing stuff. He smacked my backside, spread my butt cheeks apart, and continued to please me.

I couldn't remember if I was the soldier or the sex deprived woman. It didn't matter if Keith wanted to role-play, I was going to give him a production. Before I could

x

steal the show with my climax, he grabbed my legs and had me in a wheelbarrow position. He managed to pick me up off the dresser and lay me down on the carpet. With my knees touching my shoulders that man rocked my world. Moments into our lovemaking, I began to shake. I climaxed repeatedly and never once did Keith lose a beat. He worked my body like it was a song he was remixing. He wanted this sexcapade to be better than the one before, and it was!

"I love you," Keith said as his body collapsed on top of me.

Did I hear him right? Did Keith say he loved me? We had not been a couple for that long. I was not sure if I was in love with him. I knew for damn sure I was infatuated with him. I was truly feeling him. There was not a day that passed without me seeing him. I loved doing things with him and being around him.

Was I in love with him? My heart pounded whenever I was near him. The sound of his voice or the mention of his name put a smile on my face. I wanted nothing more than to be with him morning, noon and night. Yeah, I was in love with Keith Anthony Simmons III!

"I love you, too."

"Hey, Daddy." A little girl wearing a gorgeous black mink coat and a great big smile ran up to Keith as we walked up the stairs of a beautiful home.

Daddy? Who the hell was her daddy? I turned around to see if there was someone behind us.

Keith embraced the little girl with a great big bear hug. Why hadn't he ever mentioned to me that he had kids? From the look of the house, I expected a wife or ex-wife to come running behind her and give Keith a big kiss.

"Chante, I would like for you to meet my shining star. Chante, this is Keia." He straightened out Keia's burgundy dress underneath her coat. "And Keia, this is daddy's lady friend, Chante."

That was the second time I was referred to as a lady friend. Why couldn't I be more than a lady friend? Didn't he just tell me that he loved me? It didn't matter why I was being referred to as his lady friend, what mattered was that Keith and I had been seeing one another for almost three months. Out of thirty days in a month, Keith spent twenty of those nights with me. He had every opportunity to tell me he was someone's father.

"Hello, Keia." I gripped Keith's arm.

Keia frowned her pretty little brown face. She grabbed her father's other arm and rolled her hazel eyes. "Hey."

The look on Keith's face told me he was not pleased with the actions of his little shining star. He let go of Keia's hand and bent down to talk to her. "You both should to get used to seeing each other's pretty faces because you're going to be around each other for a while."

I, too, had a look of disgust on my face. This was not cool. It was not an issue that he had a child; however, if he had more than one I would be ready to take my I love you back. Keith knew I felt awkward and kissed me on my forehead. How was a kiss supposed to soothe me? How was a kiss going to make up for the lie that he had been keeping? Okay, it was not an actual lie. I never asked him if he had children. But, wouldn't any parent tell someone if they had children? I wanted to walk back over to the Maserati, be a big baby and say take me home.

"Ma, Ma," Keith called out as we entered the huge house.

"Whatcha keep calling me for, boy?" A medium sized woman with an apron around her waist stepped out of the kitchen into the foyer.

Keith's mother was beautiful. He looked just like her. They had the same long eyelashes and almond-shaped eyes. Mrs. Simmons' caramel-coated skin was a shade darker than Keith's. She didn't look a day over forty-eight. With so many similarities and a look of youthfulness, they looked like they could have been brother and sister rather than mother and son.

"I want you to meet my girlfriend." He blushed.

I couldn't help but smile.

"Ma, this is Chante Chambers." He turned and faced me. "And Chante, this is my mother, Rita Simmons."

She flashed me a big warm smile. She had dimples, too.

Damn, Keith and his mother both had the same smile. I looked at her and smiled back. The way Keith was grinning made me want to take him right there in his mother's living room.

"Hi, Mrs. Simmons." I couldn't stop smiling. I felt like I was in the hot seat the way everyone was staring at me.

"Hello, Chante. Call me Rita," she replied. "I've heard a lot about you."

"Chante, I like your shoes, are they Manolos?" Keia asked. "My mommy has those shoes."

The little girl shocked me. "Keia, how old are you?"

"Six," she proudly stated.

"And what do you know about Manolos?" I questioned.

"My mommy dresses cute like you. She works for *Vogue*, the magazine. I think she's a fashion editor, right, Daddy?"

Keith nodded.

She had given me a compliment. My feelings were beginning to change toward her.

"That still doesn't tell me what you know about Manolos." I smiled

"I know about Gucci, Prada. My mommy shops in Saks, Bloomies, and she loves Dolce & Gabbana."

As Keia talked about her mother, I saw the similarities between her mother and me. I had never met a six-year-old that could point out Manolos or owned a mink coat. Miss Keia was a piece of work that I could learn to like.

"My child support payments keep her shopping in those stores," Keith mumbled. "Keia, come with me. I have something for you in the car."

Keith made up some excuse about showing Keia something in the car so that his mother and I could be alone. It was time for my test.

"I'm glad to finally meet you." His mother would not stop smiling.

I followed her into the kitchen.

"The feeling is mutual." His mother was cooking cabbage, and I was tasting it.

"Keith keeps talking about you, like Ma, you have to meet this woman." His mother checked on the corn beef. "I'm not trying to be funny, but in the magazine you didn't look all that."

Keith's mother just dissed me. But it was cool because as long as she was talking and cooking, I was listening and eating.

"I think you look beautiful in person. I think that's why Keith likes you."

Being friends with nosy Kayla, I had learned when to listen and when just to nod and say, um hum. Now was the time for me to put the fork down and give Mrs. Simmons my full attention.

"Keith always liked pretty girls. You know those high yellow girls with the long hair. Nowadays everyone has a weave. Is that a weave in your hair?"

My roller set was looking great, full of body, and curls hanging inches past my shoulders, courtesy of my trip to *With a Little Jazz* that morning. I had to try to revitalize Mecca's creation after Keith grabbed it and made me sweat it out. From the looks of it, I had done a good job of fixing it.

"No, Ma'am."

"I didn't think it was." Out of the corner of my eye, I saw Rita looking me up and down and searching for tracks.

"As I was saying, Keith was always into those prissy girls. You know the kind that care more about what you can buy them, more so than actually caring about you. Like Keia's mother. That's one woman he should have left alone. I can't stand that woman. I love the grandbaby she bore me, but I can't stand her. I keep telling Keith you can't make these whores into housewives." She frowned.

"Let me tell you, Chante, I know that my son likes you a lot. He tells me *everything.*" She looked at me hard. "*Everything.* I know you two have been together for a little while, but my son is falling in love with you. He has never brought a woman around Keia.

"My son is head over heels for you, so please don't hurt him. From what I can see of you, I like you and I can understand why he likes you, too. Let me tell you I was happy to see you were brown. I need some grandbabies with color. I love Keia to death, but that little girl is lacking color."

Rita smiled at me and I flashed a phony smile. I felt so guilty for sleeping with Jason, right after I had met her son. Maybe she knew I was a whore? So, Keith was attracted to whores? I thought it was our sense of style that attracted him. How was I to know that her son had a love jones for me way before we ever met?

Rita fed us well. After I ate I had a case of niggeritis. I felt like slipping out of my dress clothes and into some sweat pants and a t-shirt. I wanted to hit the bed more than Broadway. But my man planned a night out for me to get to know the most important lady in his life, Keia. I was going to do my best to make him happy. Besides, I didn't want his mother to come hunt me down for hurting her son.

Eleven

Carol's Café was packed with the lunchtime rush. There was not an empty table in the place. Standing patrons occupied the aisles that waitresses fought through carrying trays of food. The ambience in the café was usually relaxing, or so I heard, yet today it was anything but that. I could not understand why Kayla picked this place for lunch. Yes, I could. The café was situated in Chelsea, which was a step away from the stressful and busy world of midtown Manhattan, where Jason's World and Blazing 99 resided. Carol's Cafe was perfect for lunch if you were in the mood for a sandwich; however, my mouth was craving oxtails, cabbage with red beans and rice from Maroons.

So far my day had been hectic, and it was nowhere near over. My morning consisted of an asshole trying his damndest to sell me a very weak script. The jackass would not take no for an answer, so instead I told him to fuck off. We had final call back auditions for a new pilot. My meeting with the network executives paid off. The auditions consisted of a bunch of non-actors trying to act. I wanted to scream at the casting department for bringing me such BS.

By ten-thirty I had a headache. I decided to just cancel auditions. It was very rude of me to constantly walk out of the room while people tried their best to impress me. What the hell was the purpose of me auditioning people who were not going to get the part?

By ten forty-five, my head was screaming for Excedrin. To ease my headache, I decided to outsource the job. Rosemary called up the agencies and advised them to send over their cream of the crop.

My Excedrin was not kicking in fast enough, for my emergency staff meeting. I had four weeks until production started and I had no cast. I had my lead actor although creative and development had a week, a week and half at the max to find the rest of my cast.

An hour later, I was in my office checking my email for signs of hope. What I found was an email from Keith telling me he was missing me. My reply was interrupted with an announcement that we were having problems on the set of Black's music video. My job as producer was to make sure everything that was needed was there. The house we were renting in Jersey was not up to par with Black, so at the last minute we rented the mansion next door.

Now, the video chick/actress who was Black's love interest in the video didn't want Black to feel her butt on camera. I had felt a sense of relief when Jason hired someone to run the music video division while John was locked up for tax evasion, yet Carson Reid didn't start until next week. So it was still my problem.

Personally speaking, if I was not loving Keith, I would have filled in for the, "now I have values" video chick. They wanted to be called actresses, so let me be politically correct, I would have filled in for the actress. I played the love interest in Todd's "Sweet Thing" video, so I knew what to do. Black was fine as hell, with a capital F! He was triple platinum and worth a lot to Jason. Whatever Black wanted he got. I tried my best to convince the girl to just roll with it.

"It's against my religion," she argued.

I argued, "Was it against your religion when you did it at the audition? And again during rehearsal?"

The longer she procrastinated, the more money it would cost Jason, which meant the more bullshit I would have to hear. Girls killed me with all the "I'll do this" and "I'll do that," then when they realized that their mamas was going to see what they did, all their values and home training came back. That was when it turned into "I don't do that."

I simply told the girl, "Fuck it! Don't do it. Someone else will." I picked another *actress* almost as cute as me who was more than willing to let Black feel her butt and anything else if he wanted to.

My day had turned around for the best. I was so happy to hear Kayla's voice that morning on the other end of my cell phone. I needed a break bad! I was still mad at her. Nevertheless, I missed her like crazy. She was truly sorry for airing my business on the radio, or so she had said. It was time for me to let it go, so I had accepted her apology. After fighting my way through the crowd, I saw her sitting in the back at a booth flagging me down.

Before I reached her a familiar face caught my eye. I smiled at Todd and winked. He did the nod thing that black men did as a gesture for saying what's up. His female companion, Carson Reid waved.

"Hi, Chante," Carson spoke. "I'm excited about Monday."

"Hey, Carson." *Where in the hell did Jason find this girl?*

Carson had to be dumber than a doorknob. She was pretty but stupid, your typical high yellow girl, with thick curly hair, like those twins, Tia and Tamara, besides her hair was sandy brown. Biracial, with blue eyes, Carson stood at about 5'5, an inch or two shorter than me. She was no competition for me because I was a brown skinned bombshell. I had my own real hair and you know a sistah was banging in all the right areas.

Then again, maybe she was competition? Against my better judgment, Jason pulled rank and hired the hatbox. It only meant one thing: the girl gave good head. I had to grin at that. I made a mental note to watch Miss Carson when she entered the doors of Jason's World. She had but one time to attempt to play my role. The day she did, my uppity ghetto ass was going to have to take off the Manolos and step into some Air Force Ones. It was going to be very fun working with her.

Kayla's face brightened at the sight of me. "Tae Tae, thank you for coming."
She stood and gave me a hug.

I became two shades brighter as well. "Kayla, stop acting like I am a fan or some advertiser trying to buy time." I sat. "What happened to greeting me with hey girl, what's up?"

"Hey girl, what's up," Kayla replied. "I ordered you a corn beef sandwich and a Pepsi. Is that alright?"

She knew it was all right.

"Next time I will choose where we go for lunch. Since, you don't listen."

"The wait at Maroons was too long, so there was a

change in plans. Now, shut up and tell me who the hell got you glowing?" Kayla barked.

"Damn, Kayla! Must you be so loud?" I blushed.

"Was I loud?"

"Yes, you were." I sipped her Sprite.

"Oh, I'm sorry. Last I heard from you, you were fucking a vibrator." We both laughed.

"Fuck you, Kayla."

"Must you be so blunt," she asked sarcastically.

"Yes, I must!" How was she going to get mad at me because I said fuck you, yet she just told the whole restaurant that I played with myself.

After a long pause, Kayla smiled and revisited her question. "So…who has you glowing?"

I smiled.

"Look, I am nosy. I don't have the number one morning gossip show in the New York Tri-State area for nothing. I'm going to keep asking until you tell me."

I continued to smile. She was not going to let it go. The restaurant got quieter. Everyone wanted to know who had Chante Chambers glowing, so it seemed. Todd knew for damn sure it was not him; I noticed he resumed his conversation with Carson. I waited for the restaurant to go back to minding its own business, and then I blurted it out.

"Keith Simmons." I was cheesing.

"Who is Keith Simmons?"

"My man."

Kayla's smile matched mine. "Keith from Pretty Boy Records?" She was cheesing. "I want to know how, when, why, and where." Good thing Kayla was paid to be nosy. "And when can I meet him?"

"In due time."

"Give me details."

"Kayla, that man has remixed my body in so many ways." I blushed.

"Tae Tae, you fucked him already?" Kayla always had a way of calling me a slut. If she wasn't calling me a hoe, then she was politely informing me that I gave up the butt too quickly. She was such a hypocrite. Kayla screwed Shawn the same night she met him and knew he had someone else. But that was another story.

"Yes darling, I fucked him. Numerous times. It's very good might I add." I sipped her Sprite again.

"Now if you want the 411 on my man, you have to make sure it stays off the radio."

"How many times do I have to tell you I'm sorry? You have taken our friendship away from me for three months. I have taken you out and you are still not satisfied. I told you I got the gossip from someone else at Jason's World. You know I would never go on the air and repeat something you told me." Kayla pleaded. "And you could've told me you punched Simone in the face. You know that heifer told me she walked into a wall when I asked her how she got a black eye."

We both laughed.

"Her eye looked fucked up. You know she's lighter than me."

"Well, now she knows what happens when you mess with what's mine," I said as the waitress placed my sandwich on the table.

"Chante, you and Jason are over. And have been for years."

"Kayla, it wasn't even about Jason." It was, but I couldn't tell her that. "I could care less about Jason getting his dick sucked. You didn't see what I saw when I walked in Jason's office. Your cousin straight up disrespected me. That's why I punched her in the face. And I no longer wish to talk about it."

Silence.

"Well, why did you invite Mecca to a party at Uptowns and not me?" she asked smiling. "You know she was bragging about it as soon as I walked into With a Little Jazz."

"Was she?" I took another bite of my sandwich.

"You know Mecca. She bragged about how she met this one rapper, and she met some guy from the Knicks. She hooked up with him and so forth. I just laughed in her face. She gets on my nerves bragging."

"Who are you telling?"

"Tell me about Keith."

I was planning on telling Kayla all about Mr. Simmons right after he left my house that first morning. After hearing my dirty laundry being aired on her show, I had no words for her. Keith was my business, and I was going to keep it that way.

"I met Keith at Uptowns. He invited me to his birthday party." I told Kayla all about my encounter with Keith Simmons III.

"You smoked a cigarette? When you started smoking?" She frowned.

"Kayla, it was just that good."

"Was it a good two minutes or more like an hour?"

I had eaten my corn beef sandwich. Kayla had killed her tuna fish. She had even eaten the tuna that fell off the bread with her crackers. For desert we ate strawberry cheesecake and drank cappuccinos. The check was on the table, and it was only then that I mentioned I met Keia.

"I wish a man would tell me he had a daughter damn near three months into the affair. Why didn't he tell you that on the first date? Well, y'all was too busy fucking. Ain't like you thought to ask do you have AIDS, a car, or a kid." Kayla was going eighty-five mph with her questions, and it was getting on my nerves. I felt like saying would you prefer if the kid was conceived after we were together like Shawn had done to her.

I was not going to feed into Kayla's nonsense. There was too much negativity coming from her mouth, which meant things at home were not as good as she would have liked me to believe.

"Kayla, please." I could have said things to hurt her, but what would be the point? I rolled my eyes and continued, "Anyway! Broadway was a disaster. That little girl cried about everything. Keia cried because she could not sit on the end. She cried because her father asked me to take her to the bathroom as opposed to him. She cried because I sat in the front seat next to her daddy in the car.

"She cried again because Keith took her back to Long Island, before dropping me off. That little girl left me with a damn headache. I mean she was a real pain in the ass, and Keith knew it. I don't know what made him think that after our evening, I was going to take him home with me."

"Why would he think differently?" Kayla mumbled.

Deep breath in. Deep breath out. With closed eyes, I inhaled and then exhaled. I cleared my mind and did it once again. Lord knew I did not want to fight with Kayla again. If she had problems she should just voice them as opposed to killing my joy.

"I didn't think Keith and I were going to see another date after that night," I said. "The next day he came and got me for breakfast with the brat in the car. And I knew it was going to be *The Lion King* all over again. Keith told me that after a talk and a spanking, Keia fell in line.

"She even apologized. Kayla, you should have seen her. She's a very pretty little girl. That little girl knew I had on Manolos." I took a breath. "She said, 'Miss Chante, I'm sorry I messed up you and my daddy's date' and gave me a hug. Maybe she was playing me. Personally I didn't care. I am loving her daddy. That little girl wasn't going to run me off that easily."

Kayla's eyes and attention trailed off as I spoke. The same smile that graced her face at the beginning of our conversation was long gone. She grunted and rolled her eyes a few times as well. While I spoke, she was not listening. She shrugged in a gesture to say whatever.

She rolled her eyes and then she spoke, "So what are you

doing?"

"What do you mean?" My face was blank. I had no idea what she was asking.

"Are y'all, just fucking, kicking it for a minute or what?"

"Kayla, the man washed me up." I closed my eyes and envisioned the evening in my bathroom all over again. "We didn't have sex. He washed me up like I was a goddess. You know how the bathers washed Eddie Murphy up in *Coming to America*?"

"And?" She rolled her eyes again.

For the third time, I ignored her and proceeded to explain. "He washed me, then applied lotion to my skin. As I dressed in the bedroom, he played the piano and serenaded me." I heard the song Keith played for me in my head.

"And you're in love." A phony smile spread across her face.

First the heifer ruined my reminiscing, ignored me while I was speaking, and now she was acting like she cared. Kayla always had a way of stealing my joy. I understood why so many of her listeners called her a hater. Kayla was the only one who could be in love. Only Kayla could be happy. If Chante was happy, or Chante was in love, then Chante had to be thinking with her pussy. Only Kayla could be lucky enough to find her knight in shiny armor; too bad his broke ass came along with baby mama drama.

"Don't rain on my parade. If I am happy allow me to be happy, and be happy for me." I never questioned my friendship with Kayla. I had known her for over twenty years and could not imagine life without her. Yet, at this point I was contemplating doing just that. The longer I looked at her, the more I realized why I never returned any of her phone calls over the past few months.

"Kayla, for once *be* my friend." The words were uttered slowly. Slow enough for Kayla to seep it all in. "For once, *be* my friend," I repeated.

"Aren't we sensitive?" Kayla realized she had pinched a nerve. But her words didn't prove she cared.

Ten minutes went by and nothing was said. I picked at my second piece of cheesecake, while only the crumbs of Kayla's third slice remained. She stuck her fork in my cake and began to eat it. I shook my head and slid the entire plate over to her. Kayla was turning into a fucking pig. Kayla had always been a glamour girl.

Her style was simple, yet, elegant and expensive. Today, my best friend was dressed in a style of someone else. Today she was anything but fabulous. She wore jeans, a pair of Timberlands and a t-shirt that read 'I have issues'. That she did. Her leather jacket added a little style along with a long red scarf. Her hair was pulled back in a ponytail. Her yellow face was bland, no color, artificial or otherwise, not even lip-gloss. She looked sick. She pissed me off the way she ate the tuna fish sandwich. With every bite she scoffed down, my face had a different disgusted expression.

"Go ahead tell me about your man." Kayla had actually made time to stop devouring the cake to speak.

"I am in love. It's the first time in a long time." I smiled.

Once again Kayla was doing her best job of ignoring me. "Chante, cut him loose now."

"Why would you say that?" I was ready to kick her ten pound overweight ass. This was the first feeling of love I had since Jason and she was killing it. Before I proceeded to punch her, I was willing to hear her out. She knew gossip, maybe she knew something I didn't know.

"He's a liar." She pointed her fork at me. "How can someone lie about having a child and tell you months later? What kind of shit is that?"

"Why don't you ask Shawn how one can do that?" I put forty dollars on the table and rose. "Ask that motherfucker why the hell he can't keep his dick to himself. You ask the man you love, and maybe you'll get the answer to your question."

The restaurant once again turned silent. I had no time to notice that all eyes were on us. I was too busy walking away and putting on my winter white cashmere coat.

"Chante, wait," Kayla yelled as I walked out the door.

"Go to hell!" I was gone.

"Taxi. Taxi." Black men found it hard to get a cab in New York City. Well, this black woman was having a hard time trying to flag one down as well.

"Chante," Kayla called.

At the sound of her voice, I started walking down West 25th Street. I wanted to be as far away from Kayla as I could. I swore to God I did not want to fight my best friend. The way she made me feel I wanted to slap the shit out of her.

"Chante." Her fat ass followed me.

"Kayla, leave me the hell alone." I crossed 8th Avenue. Kayla was close behind.

"Would you stop? I can't walk that fast," she yelled.

I ignored her and continued to walk.

"I'm pregnant," she blurted out.

I stopped walking but did not turn around. "Am I supposed to be happy for a friend who can't be happy for me?"

"Chante, please hear me out. I'm sorry," she pleaded as she stepped closer to me.

"Congratulations," I said with sarcasm.

"Don't congratulate me. I'm not having that bastard's baby."

I should have known. The argument Kayla and I just had was not about me. She was not listening to me because she was too busy dealing with her own relationship. I knew home wasn't a happy place for her. That was the reason she could not be happy for me. She tried. At the beginning of our conversation, she was into what I had to say, but quickly her interest had vanished.

"Chante, I am sorry about lunch. It was not my intention for it to go there. I tried to get my mind off of Shawn and his dirty dick ass." The words 'dirty dick' were squeezed out through clenched teeth. "I'm sorry."

"Apology accepted." I did not have time for Kayla and Shawn's drama. I had an afternoon meeting with my production crew, and I had open call auditions at three.

Kayla had known Shawn was a dog from the day she met him. Afterwards she had various run-ins with his whores and firsthand knowledge of his infidelities, but she always went back to him.

I did not have to turn around and look at Kayla to know that she was crying. There was no reason for me to be happy about her pregnancy because she was not happy. Kayla was my sister, and I could feel her pain.

"Kayla, what do you want me to do?"

"I want you to help me put him out."

"And how do you suppose I can help you do that?" I asked, stopping in the middle of the street.

I already knew the answer. I had been down this road before. A long time ago, I traveled down the street where I threw all of Kayla's belongings into Gucci carry-on bags and suitcases while she hid in the bathroom. I knocked on the door three times to let her know that I had broken up with Shawn for her and then we left. This time it would be slightly different since he was the one being evicted.

"Look, Kayla, I can't go anywhere right now I have auditions in about thirty minutes. You can come with me to the auditions, or we can meet up later and I'll help you."

"Thanks."

"You're welcome." A cab finally stopped for me.

Kayla smiled from ear to ear. "Tae Tae, one more favor."

I knew she wanted something else.

"Yes, Kayla," I said getting in the cab.

"Can you please give Simone a role in something?" She was begging. The child must have been smoking crack if she thought I was going to give that slut anything.

"HELL NAW!" I said it how Sophia had responded in *The Color Purple* when the white lady asked her to be her maid. "Did you forget we caught that little cunt sucking Jason's dick? Did you forget my fist was the wall she walked into?"

"By the way, that was her who called up to the station,"

she said.

I nodded my head because I had pretty much figured that out.

"Come on, Chante." Kayla knocked on the window. "I want her out my house, and without a job where is she going to go?"

I looked at Kayla and smiled. "Not my problem."

"Look, she needs to go.

I just smiled at Kayla and told the cabbie to pull away.

As soon as the Bentley Continental GT pulled into her driveway, Kayla was standing in the garage motioning for me to hurry up. She'd practically opened the car door and pulled me out of the car.

"Kayla, what's the matter? What's the rush?" I asked trying to get the key out of the ignition.

She placed her finger over her mouth to shush me while she dragged me into the house via the garage.

"Who are you on the phone with?" I asked, closing the garage door.

She took the phone off of her ear and held it against her thigh. "Didn't I say shut up?"

I gave Kayla the 'I will smack the shit out of you' look. Simone looked up from painting her toenails and giggled at my expression.

"Hey, Chante." She smirked.

"How's the eye?" I winked and followed Kayla. As we walked up the stairs, she handed me the other cordless phone.

"Tae Tae," Once again Kayla took the phone off her ear as she sat down on the wine-colored couch. "Can you believe that motherfucker has the audacity to be on the phone with *his* woman in *my* house?"

"Kayla, why are you listening to him talk to her on the phone?" I asked, taking my jacket off. I couldn't understand why she still had her jacket on, along with her sunglasses.

"Press mute at the same time you press talk so they don't hear us."

What in the hell was wrong with my friend?

I just stared at Kayla like she was crazy. She pressed mute and the talk button at the same time and handed me the telephone. I could not believe we were sitting on the couch listening to her man talk on the phone with another woman like they were teenagers in love. He was not worth it. Shawn suffered from DDD, Dirty Dick Disease. For some reason, he couldn't seem to shake the disease. After the first symptoms, Kayla sat him down and had a talk with him. When his whore knocked on his door at two in the morning, Kayla tried to handle the situation. She ended up with a black eye.

There was no way in hell I was going to have my high yellow friend walking around with a black eye. We were too cute for that. I did what any good friend would have done. I went to the woman's house and blackened both of her eyes. A month later, Shawn was still cheating with the same woman. This went on for a while. Too long if you asked me. Once Tasha popped up pregnant, the fight was over. As far as I was concerned, Tasha could have Shawn's behind. But no, Kayla still wanted her man.

I didn't know what Kayla saw in him. Yeah, he was handsome, cinnamon brown with sandy brown curly hair and eyes that switched from hazel to gray and on some days blue with the weather. According to Kayla, in the bedroom he was as good as they come. He taught sixth grade at one of New York City's public schools. If you asked me, those were his three best assets. He was handsome, the sex was good, and he had a job.

I understood why the average woman would keep Shawn's philandering ass. But Kayla was not the average woman. She was beautiful. She made six figures while Shawn barely made five. I don't know how he managed to woo my Gucci loving friend.

"Kayla, I cannot believe you want to sit here and listen to this." My face showed disgust. "You got to be hurting listening to this crap."

As I looked to my right at my sister, her shades could not hide the tears. I wrapped my arms around her and held her.

"Kayla, why do you do this to yourself?" I asked as I let go.

"Chante, I love that man."

"Do you think he has you on his brain right now?"

"It doesn't matter, Chante. It's his child growing inside of me. This is the man I'm supposed to marry." She pointed to the diamond ring that Shawn was still paying for as the tears poured down her face.

"Why? Because he asked you to marry him?" I asked. "Kayla, do you think I should have married Jason despite the fact that he cheated on me numerous times, and I caught him?"

"Well….you could've tried to work it out."

I looked at her like she was stupid.

"Work out what? You tried to work it out how many times and what did you get? What did you get, damn it?" I wanted her to answer me. I wanted her to think back to all the shit she had been through with Shawn and his cheating. She needed to see that all of this wasn't worth it.

Her tears answered my question.

Enough was enough.

"Kayla, is this what he does?" I took the phone from her and hung up. "He sits in *your* house on *your* phone while you are home and talk to his women?"

She wiped her face. "He doesn't know I'm home."

"So does that make it right?" I stood. "Where is he?"

"In the den."

As I journeyed down the long hallway, I could hear Shawn on the phone still talking to his mistress. In between the laughter, he told her how he couldn't wait to hold her in his arms again. Through the crack in the door, I could see Shawn relaxed on the couch. His arms were stretched out, feet up on the coffee table while a sandwich and soda sat on it.

"Get the fuck out!" I said as I busted open the door.

Shawn twisted his head to the side and looked at me with a perplexed look.

"I said get the fuck out!" I snatched the phone and hung it up.

"Come on, Chante, don't start this shit." Shawn knew what time it was.

"You have some fucking nerve."

"What are you talking about?" Shawn asked.

I ignored him. Instead I answered the ringing phone, "Hello?"

Shawn's mistress called back. "Can I speak to Shawn?"

"No. And please do not call here again."

"Is this Kayla?"

"Does it matter who the fuck it is? You were asked nicely not to call here again. Now you can either follow directions, or you can continue to piss me off and then take the ass whooping that comes next."

"Look, Boo Boo, take it down a notch. Just tell Kayla her bedroom is nicely decorated. However I would've hung different drapes." She hung up.

"You brought that bitch into my home?" Kayla flew past me with the phone still in her hand.

She jumped on Shawn and proceeded to slap and punch him. I contemplated helping her jump him. Shawn was dead wrong this time. However, Kayla was pregnant and although she said she wasn't going to have the baby, I knew that wasn't the truth. Just like I knew she wasn't serious about putting him out.

"Kayla!" I attempted to pull her off. Instead she pushed me away.

"Kayla, you are pregnant!" I said pulling her by her shirt collar.

"Shawn, how could you bring that woman into my house? How could you do this to me?" I held my best friend while she cried like a baby.

Shawn sat on the couch with his head in his hands looking like a dumbass.

"Kayla, fuck him," I said consoling my friend and staring her baby's father in his eyes.

"Bitch," Shawn mumbled.

"Who are you calling a bitch? Me? Your pregnant fiancé? Or the whore you were on the phone with?" I let go of Kayla.

"Tae Tae, won't you go home and mind your own fucking business." He rose.

"My name has always been Chante to you. As long as I am alive, Kayla will always be my business because I love her. And I care about her unlike your nasty ass."

"Pregnant?" Shawn questioned, following Kayla out of the den and up the stairs.

"Leave me alone, Shawn." Kayla walked into their bedroom straight toward Shawn's closet.

"Kayla, you're pregnant?"

"Shawn, leave my house."

He grabbed her arm.

"If you don't get your hands off of my friend, I will knock you the hell out," I said looking around for something to hit him with.

He let go.

"This belongs to you?" She handed him her ring.

"Why didn't you tell me that you were pregnant?"

"Shawn, would it have made a difference?" Kayla pushed him. "Would it have stopped you from talking to that woman on my phone? I want to know what in the hell possessed you to bring that bitch into my house? Into my bed?" She punched him in his chest.

"I hate your ass." She slapped him in the face. "I have

loved your tired ass for too goddamn long and look at how you treat me. What do these skanks do for you that I don't? Not a damn thing because I do it all. And this is how you repay me. I am officially tired." Kayla's right hand touched his jaw for the second time.

Shawn was lot of things, but a woman beater he was not. He took his hits like a man. He shook his head and mumbled some obscenities when I handed him a garbage bag to put his things in while I packed another.

"Make sure you leave the keys on your way out."

"I'm not going anywhere."

I stood between him and Kayla. "Kayla heard you on the phone with that girl. She heard your entire conversation. She had me listening to it. Then to make matters worse, the bitch called back, which means you don't respect Kayla enough to have the chick call you on your cell phone.

"That heifer calls on the house phone. The bitch told me to tell Kayla her bedroom is nicely decorated. How the hell would she know that? I felt like crying listening to you tell that woman how you love her, and Kayla gets on your nerves and she's this and she's that."

"Shawn, you have disrespected me for the last time. You got to go!" Kayla screamed.

I smirked, handing him his garbage bag. "Like I said, leave the keys on your way out."

Twelve

Jodeci's "Feenin'" was in surround sound throughout my condo. I sang along. I even added my own twist. A sistah was craving some loving badly! It was hot and I was horny. There was no reason for the central air to be on, especially not in November, yet I had it on high. Nothing was working for my rising temperature. These last five nights had been very lonely for me. Even though I knew he was away on business, I missed Keith. I could go without sex for breakfast and lunch. However, a sistah had to be put to bed right. Lord knew after the drama with Kayla, I needed a hug. I needed to feel loved, and I needed a massage. I needed my man.

That felt so good to say. I had a man! Forget Jodeci, I started singing "Chante's Got a Man." Well, he wasn't at home with me. I wished he was, but I would just have to improvise like I had done last night.

Last night I pretended Keith parted my thighs in the middle of the night. His lips said goodnight to my love palace with a nice long passionate kiss. His hands played with every entrance on my body.

Tonight we would try something a little different. On my way back to Jason's World from lunch, I stopped in one of the few sex shops in Times Square that Giuliani had not closed down. I bought this contraption called a love machine. It cost me too much money but according to the box it was worth it.

Just as I plugged up my love machine and put myself in my position of choice, on all fours, the damn phone rang. I let it ring. I backed up onto my love machine. Inside I felt sensations coming from all over. I hoped this thing didn't electrocute me.

With closed eyes, I backed my thang up. I bit my bottom lip and grabbed the carpet. Within five minutes I was moaning. Next thing I knew I was singing Keith's name.

It was day eight. Keith had only been gone for one week and a day. He would be away for another two or three weeks. What was I going to do? I was like a drug addict in need of a hit. How was I going to cope without my baby for another two weeks while he handled some business on the other side of the country? Last week, he worked the Midwest and the west coast; this week he would be in the dirty south. The week after that he still wouldn't be with me.

I hated to bother my man while he did business, but I was at the point where I was tempted to order a plane ticket to Texas so I could meet up with him and be in his presence. I thought I would be able to do it, but I couldn't go without sex. Maybe it was because I had went so long without it before, that once my body was reintroduced to it, it decided we weren't giving it up ever again.

The love machine was money well spent, but it was not Keith. I did the good girlfriend thing while he was gone. I gave Keia's mother a break and took Keia for Keith's weekend. I was so glad that the weekend was over. Over the three and a half months that I had known Keith, I had grown to love Keia. She was a little me, which meant her mama and me had too much in common other than the obvious; we had both made love to Keith. Keia was a bit fresh with me, yet once she found out I was not going anywhere and I didn't hesitate to spank her butt, her freshness ceased.

After dropping Keia off, I did a little shopping to get my mind off of Keith. It didn't really help. I brought two pairs of boots, a pair of bad ass shoes and some clothes, but the majority of my shopping spree was spent at *La Perla's* on lingerie.

Not only did I miss Keith's sex, I missed his conversation and more importantly, I missed his company. As soon as I walked into my condo, I felt his presence. I dropped my coat on the floor and kicked my shoes off somewhere in the living room. The bathtub was calling me.

A nice hot bubble bath always did the trick of relaxing me, but tonight it was not working. I slipped on a pair of pink lace boy cut briefs that I had just bought since I was feeling sexy and lied down on the chaise to watch some television.

"What's up, baby?" I was so happy to hear Keith's voice on the other end of the phone.

"Hey, Babe," I responded.

"Did I wake you?" He was so caring and sensitive. I loved that.

The time on the cable box read 12:35 a.m.

"You know I never mind you waking me up for anything." I was happy to hear Keith's voice on the other end of the phone. His voice was turning me on.

"I called you last night. Why didn't you answer the phone?"

"Baby, I was knocked out."

"I thought maybe you went out. Next time I call, you better answer the phone if you are there."

"And what if I am sleep?"

"I'm worth waking up for."

I smiled. He was right. He was worth it.

"Are you in Texas yet?"

"No, I'm still on the tour bus, but I didn't call you to talk about that."

"What do you want to talk about?"

"You."

"Oh really, what about me would you like to talk about?" I smiled.

"What did you do today?"

"Me and Keia went shopping."

"And was my angel on her best behavior?"

"You know I was."

"My other angel."

"Keia was Keia."

"That's good to hear."

"How was your day?"

"Fine and yours?"

"My day was okay, but it was missing something."

"What was it missing?"

"You."

"I missed you, too, Baby."

"You naked?"

"Partially."

I felt a smile spread across Keith's face. "Touch your breast."

I did as I was told.

"I love how it feels when I pull your nipples between my fingers."

"I do, too."

"Can you do that for me?"

"Keith, I will do anything you ask."

"Kiss them for me."

I did.

My phone rang again, and I thought it was Keith calling back for round two. Instead, it was the night doorman telling me I had a visitor.

I must have been knocked out because I couldn't recall George saying who was at my door. Keith must have lied. He wasn't on a tour bus to Texas instead he was on a red eye flight to Newark Liberty Airport. Who else would be visiting me at this time of night?

My smile vanished at the site of my unwanted visitor.

"What the hell do you want, Jason?" I folded my arms in front of my breast.

"Damn you look good." I bet I did standing there topless.

"What are you doing here?" I couldn't believe my eyes.

"Chante, I love you." I tasted the alcohol on his breath when his lips pressed against mine, and his tongue moved around in my mouth.

I tried to push Jason away, but his finger felt so good in my love palace. His tongue was no longer in my mouth; it was slowly moving down my neck and on to my breast.

Chante. Chante. Chante! What in the hell are you doing? My eyes were closed and my neck was rolling around enjoying the chills that Jason was sending down my spine. My hands traced his body.

"I love you, Tae Tae." He kissed my lips. "I never meant to hurt you." He dropped to his knees and began to lick the palace.

Just then "I Wanna Love You" by Donell Jones played on the quiet storm. I had left the stereo on prior to falling asleep, and although the volume was low, it seemed like as soon as the song came on the volume got louder. I found myself telling Jason I wanted to love him. I dropped to my knees so that we could be face to face. Jason brushed my hair out of my face and kissed me.

"Chante, I want to try this again."

I kissed him. At that moment I was not thinking about Keith. I waited years to hear the words Jason had uttered. All I could think about was feeling Jason inside of me. Without any protection, I straddled him and put him inside of me.

In the morning, I knew I had fucked up badly. Jason made it all worth it. My thighs rested on Jason's shoulders as he proceeded to send me into convulsions. When the explosions came, Jason removed his penis and replaced it with his tongue. I almost died.

Thirteen

What was I doing? Jason was standing butt naked with his back to me using my bathroom. I admired the body of the god who just loved a sister right while Keith was on the other end of the phone I held. I was supposed to be listening to my man tell me about his day. However, listening was the farthest thing from my mind. I said, "uh hum," at the appropriate times and continued to admire Jason's behind. The sexiest thing on a man to me had always been the back. It had me grinning from ear to ear.

As Keith talked, I lay back on the chaise and watched Jason wash his hands. My nipples hardened. I wasn't sure if Keith's words caused the girls to rise since he changed the nature of our conversation or if I was having aftershocks from the earthquake Jason had just caused minutes ago in the love below.

I should've stopped Jason when he came and kneeled down next to me. I should've slapped his hand away when he untied the bow that created the keyhole in my nightshirt, but I didn't. I allowed him to pull one of the girls out and kiss her. I didn't fight him when he tongue kissed the other twin. I just kept on saying "Um hum" when appropriate. As soon as Keith told me to hold on, my lips were touching Jason's lips.

"You hear that," Keith asked, referring to the music playing in the background.

"Is that Luther?" I moved my arm so that Jason wouldn't take the phone.

In the background I heard Luther asking someone if she remembered something, and something about it being alright. Keith knew I liked this song. He turned the volume up louder and began to sing. Now was not the time for him to serenade me.

Keith, Baby, please hang up.

My head rocked to the music. I didn't know if it was the words of Luther sung by Keith that had me rocking or if it was the rhythm Jason's tongue had created.

"Can I call you back?" It was hard to speak clearly.

"Why?"

"Because someone is knocking at the door," I lied.

"I can hold on," Keith replied.

"No, you can't. Kayla and Shawn are beefing again." I made up a quick and believable lie.

"Tell Kayla I said what's up."

"Alright. I'll do that."

"I love you."

I hung up.

"Who was that on the phone?" Jason asked, lying next to me on the chaise, satisfied that he made me scream his name for the second time that afternoon.

"Who was what?" I asked in a daze.

"You have an orgasm, and you get dumb now?"

Who the hell did Jason think he was talking to? I looked at him like he was stupid.

"That's alright. We both know whose name you just screamed." He stood. "And it wasn't that nigga on the phone."

As I heard the water hit the tub from the shower, I wished the other night never happened and that Jason would go down the drain with the water. What had I started? How had I gone from that one little slip up to still screwing Jason on a full time basis? Everything Jason said the other night, he claimed he actually meant. As proof, he had been by my side these last few weeks. We went to work together, came home together and had the best sex ever each and every night. I just kept telling myself it was someone to screw while Keith was gone. Who was I convincing? Not even my damn self. I was catching feelings. I had already had feelings for Jason. I loved the arrogant bastard in my shower.

I also loved Keith.

Come on, Chante, there is no future with Jason.

Jason was just a good lay. A very good lay.

Maybe this time things would be different. Jason promised me that he would never hurt me again. He loved me. He wanted to start over. So far he was doing good.

What about Keith?

What about him?

"Hel-lo," I answered the phone.

"What are you doing?" Keith asked.

"Masturbating," I lied. I was lying in the middle of my bed with my legs spread wide open while Jason was banging my back out.

I shouldn't have answered my ringing phone. Yet, how could I explain to my man why I wasn't home at 4:14 in the morning? As soon as I saw his name and number appear on the Caller ID, I immediately answered the phone.

"Oh, looks like I called at a good time." I felt him smile. Inside I was crying. "Take all your clothes off and get butt naked."

I bopped Jason in the head, motioning him to stop. He didn't. He really began to put it on me.

"Get off the phone," he said, making his voice heard.

"Who was that?" Keith asked.

"Nobody, I'm watching a porno." I was becoming a good liar.

Keith spoke sex through the phone while Jason dicked a sistah down!

"OOHH," I moaned into the phone as my leg shook.

Jason kissed my lips and wiped the tears that were streaming down my face.

"I love you," I said to Jason.

"I love you, too," Keith replied. "I can't wait to see you on Wednesday."

"Me, too." I hung up the phone.

Fourteen

I stepped off a plane at the Miami International Airport in a Jason paid for outfit. Nothing felt as good close to your skin like Prada. From the orange sweater that tied around my neck, to the white button down shirt, down to my black capris and my sandals, I was looking like a spokesperson for Prada. My sunglasses sat on top of my head waiting for me to pull them down at the first sight of sun. As soon as I exited the gate, I felt the stares. Only one stare mattered. The dimples on my man greeted me as did his open arms. Our smiles matched each other from ear to ear. He embraced me tightly. That's when it all hit me.

What in the hell had I been doing? For the past three weeks, had I not been Jason's girlfriend? Now, here I was in the arms of the man who loved me and whom I claimed to love. I sat on the phone with my man and allowed him to hear the moans my other man had caused. My conscience started calling me all kinds of names like whore, slut, hoe, jezebel, and harlot. I was one of those women whom I despised. I was the other woman whom Kayla would kill if she caught Shawn with his pants down again. My mother had not raised me to share my pussy with two men. However, once again, here I was with my face nestled in the chest of one of the gorgeous men that I loved.

Now was not the time for me to think about my whoring. With a blink of an eye, thoughts of being a jezebel vanished. There would be plenty of time, after I returned to Jersey to think about my status as a whore. Right now I was going to concentrate on spending my first Thanksgiving with Keith. Especially after he had rearranged some things just so we could spend Thanksgiving together.

"I take it you've missed me." I was referring to the hardness rubbing against my crotch.

"Yeah, he missed you." Keith grinned and squeezed me tighter. "I missed you, too."

I felt like saying 'well, baby, mama's been doing the damn thing since you left.' I was not up for sex just yet. During these past few weeks, Jason had been servicing a sistah on the regular. After all he *was* my man, and I *was* his girl. After the phone sex thing with Keith, while Jason and I having sex, I knew it was time to end it. For the last three days I had a brother on punishment with hopes that my love palace would tighten up. I even went as far as visiting that freak store again to purchase coochie-tightening cream.

"Do you see your luggage?" Keith asked at baggage claim.

"The *Louis* collection right there." I pointed to my luggage.

"How long are you planning on staying?" Keith asked as he carried one suitcase and pulled the other one on wheels. "Do you plan on finishing the tour with me?"

I smiled, wrapped my arm tighter around his. "I'll stay for as long as you want me to."

Keith arranged lunch on the beach, which I enjoyed. Following lunch, we laid in hammocks as our food digested. He had an obsession with penthouse suites because we were rooming in one at the Palms South Beach. There was a trail of rose petals from the entrance of the suite leading to the master bedroom. The trail looked like a rose petal runner. Inside the bathroom candles were lit, their flames casting a wonderful silhouette. A bubble bath was drawn. I turned around and behind me Keith stood naked.

All I could do was smile. He had it all planned out, how he was about to devour me. He placed his finger under my chin and raised my face to his. Our lips pressed against one another. I said a silent prayer to the Lord to ensure that Keith would not fall in when he entered me. My tongue played with his as he untied my sweater. I stood still as he unbuttoned my shirt.

I rolled my head back as his tongue ran across my nipple. Goosebumps appeared, and chills went through my body as Keith placed my 36 C into his mouth. He unzipped my capris at the side. My panties fell down in unison. There I stood butt naked in a pair of Prada sandals with both of my breasts in Keith's mouth. I didn't know if we were going to make it to the tub.

My palace was throbbing for Keith to enter it. The throne was craving for him to get close to it, approach it, touch it, and keep on touching it. I backed Keith up against the wall and threw my right leg up. I looked like a ballerina doing a split in the air because my leg was straight up. Keith entered my body and once again I was in paradise with the man I loved.

I left Miami with a smile on my face. It was the best five days of my life. Keith made love to me every day of my visit. Occasionally we made it out of the hotel suite. On one occasion we went outside to the hammocks and just enjoyed the scenery and napped. All I wanted to do was be in Keith's presence. I didn't give a damn what we did. We went snorkeling, sailing, shopping, and clubbing.

For Thanksgiving, I could not have asked for anything more. I was dressed to kill in a sexy lavender Ralph Lauren number. Keith, too, looked sharp as ever in a black suit. His silk tie matched my dress. We met up with everyone from Pretty Boy Records and ate dinner together as one big ole Pretty Boy family in the hotel's restaurant.

R&B star and Pretty Boy's recording artist, Chauncey had flown in his girlfriend and their son. While Grammy award winner Sasha had flown in a man that Keith later informed me was not her husband. A table that was set for 50 was filled with wives, girlfriends, boyfriends, mistresses, children, and dates for the night.

Keith missed Keia, I could tell by the way he looked at Chauncey and his son. As decided by the courts, he would have Keia for Christmas since her mother had her for Thanksgiving. I tried my best to help him ignore everyone else there and concentrate on me. In my head, Keith and I were the only two at that table.

For the next three days, Keith rocked my world, mentally and physically, like there was no tomorrow. My man made sure he sent a sistah home with enough sex to make it through until Thursday, when he would be home.

That morning I didn't want to say goodbye, neither did Keith. We ate breakfast together on the terrace of the penthouse suite. Keith arranged for his and her massages, also on the terrace. I was beginning to think he wasn't going to let me leave. But he did.

"I want you to leave relaxed," he said as he kissed my forehead and untied my robe after our massages.

"I want to be relaxed," I responded and began to massage him.

My smile, thoughts, and memories vanished at the sight of Jason waiting for me at baggage claim at Newark Liberty Airport. *Who in the hell told him to meet me here?* I kept forgetting that Jason was my boyfriend. Quickly, I turned my head, so that he wouldn't see me looking at him. My plan was to walk right pass him like I had not seen him at all.

"Chante, over here," he called out.

"Damn." I flashed a phony smile.

He kissed me. His lips felt good pressed up against mine. *Chante, we just left Keith. We love him, remember? Yeah, but we keep forgetting we are also in a relationship with Jason.*

"How was Miami?" Jason asked taking my luggage from me. "Did you and Kayla do it up in the M-I-A?"

I lied. I told Jason, Kayla and I were going to Miami to get her mind off of Shawn. I knew she wouldn't be on the radio for Thanksgiving and that they would be playing the best of shows. And if he had heard her this morning on the radio, I had planned to tell him that she flew back yesterday because she had to do the show today.

"Yeah, we had fun."

"Where's Kayla?" Jason searched for her.

"She flew back yesterday." I was thinking of ways to ditch him. "Jason, you didn't have to come all the way here to get me. I can get a cab."

"Ain't nothing, Tae Tae." He looked at me with sex in his eyes. "I know you need what Daddy got."

He wrapped his arm around my neck. "I missed you." He kissed me again.

There was no way I was going to have sex with Jason. I was satisfied. These last five days gave me time to think, put things in perspective, and evaluate my relationships. I loved Jason. I also loved Keith. Being with Keith reminded me of why I fell in love with him. I was not willing to give him up for anything.

"How do you know I need what you have?" I asked as he put my luggage in the back of his Range Rover.

"Tae Tae, when's the last time you sat on daddy's dick? I know you need it." He smirked.

It was shit like that, that turned me off completely. I frowned.

"It sounds more like you need it. I'm straight, so Daddy can keep his dick to himself," I said as I opened the passenger side door.

"You drive," Jason said handing me the keys.

"Come on, what the hell is the problem!" Traffic was ridiculous. I was suffering from a case of road rage.

"Calm down," Jason said, brushing my hair out of my face.

"Shut up, Jason. This is why you should've driven." I smacked his hand off of my thigh. "You knew there was traffic, that's why you told me to drive."

"This is ridiculous!" Once again I was referring to traffic. Once again I knocked Jason's hand off my thigh. "Jason, would you quit it."

His hand was under my skirt searching to see if the palace guard was on duty. He found out it was. I have been known not to wear panties from time to time. Today, I had some on; however, yesterday, I did not.

A smile crept up on my face at the thought of going out to dinner with Keith last night with no panties on. My smile spread even wider at the thought of just being in the company of my man. I busted out laughing with the memory of him fingering me right at the table.

"What you over there smiling and laughing at?" Jason asked.

"Nothing," I lied. "Jason, please stop touching me."

"Why can't I touch you? It's mine. You're my girlfriend, right?" He was mad.

Jason, I was meaning to talk to you about that. I'm Keith's girlfriend.

"It's not yours. It's mine."

"I paid for the shit. It's mine."

Did that bastard just refer to me as a whore?

"You know what, Jason? Fuck you! I am going to stop getting mad at you every time you say something stupid because you don't know any better."

For the rest of the ride home, I ignored Jason. As far as I was concerned, we were through. I would bet money on that.

♫

If I had placed that bet, I would have lost my money. Jason's tongue felt good moving inside my mouth. My right breast was in the palm of his hand. He fumbled around under my shirt trying to unsnap my bra.

"Forget it," he said and just pulled my bra on top of my breast to play with my nipples.

I should have at least motioned for Jason to take the party upstairs to my condo since it was too hot and heavy outside of his Range Rover in the parking garage. I prayed none of my neighbors entered the garage. Nonetheless, even if they had, I would have said, 'Hello, Mr. or Miss whoever' and continued to get my freak on.

"Wait a minute." I pushed Jason back as I slid my thong down over my boot.

My stomach rested against the back of the Range. My left breast was in Jason's left hand while my right breast was in his other hand. My hands were planted on the truck as I braced myself for impact. I didn't give a damn if Jason fell in the palace. I didn't care if he found out that I had been screwing every day in Miami. I was pretty sure he knew I was in Miami with a man, the same man who I was on the phone with while we had had sex. Jason wasn't stupid. He knew Kayla hadn't gone with me to Miami. He was just playing my little game.

I took a deep breath as Jason entered me. I was prepared for him to do the damn thing. He tried to put it on me as if he knew my palace had had a visitor. I didn't give a damn what he knew or thought he knew. With every pump I put my back into it. Jason tried to give me all he had.

He was trying to compete with the lover I had in Miami. But there was no comparison. He was pushing for my lungs, yet he was not hitting any of my spots. He came close, but he never hit that button that made it pour down raining. I wanted to start singing Keisha Cole's hit, "I Just Want It to Be Over." I pulled my leg up, rested my leather boot on the bumper and continued to pop that thang with hopes of this episode being over soon.

♫

"Behind the Range Rover, I fucked Jason," I blurted out. I had to tell someone. I picked up the phone as soon as I walked my wet ass into the house. I dialed Kayla. After two rings I hung up. I couldn't tell her I just cheated on my boyfriend for the one-millionth time. I damn sure couldn't tell her I had screwed Jason in the parking garage where everyone could see. I could not tell her that I then walked to the front of the truck and laid on the hood as he slurped up my juices.

How the hell could I explain how I went from ignoring everything that came out of Jason's mouth to screwing him outside on his truck, like I didn't have a home or money for a hotel room. I dialed Kayla's number again. I had to tell somebody, who else was I going to tell that I just spent five beautiful days in the arms of the man I loved, to come home and have sex with Jason. I cheated and the sex wasn't even all that good. I received more pleasure from his tongue than from the stroking he was doing. Simone answered the phone. I hung up.

I could've spoken to Simone. That whore would have understood. She probably would have shared experiences. I needed someone to talk to, but I wasn't that desperate to share my business with her.

I dialed my friend Yolanda's phone number. She would understand. Afterwards, she would call me a big slut and then ask whose sex was the best. That damn Yolanda wasn't home, and neither was Mecca.

"Hello," I answered the ringing phone. I was hoping Mecca had seen my number on her Caller ID and called me back.

"Chante," It was Kayla. "What's the matter?"

How the hell did she know? "What makes you think something is wrong?"

"You have called here twice and hung up. So what's the matter?"

She didn't know. I wiped the sweat from my forehead. "Nothing's wrong."

"So what did you want?"

I just wanted to tell you that I spent five beautiful days with Keith in Miami. Jason met me at the airport, and we had sex on the hood of his car. By the way before I went to Miami, Jason and I got back together. "I called to tell you something, but I forgot whatever it was. That was why I kept hanging up."

"Oh, Okay. Well I'll talk to you later."

"All right, bye," I heard Kayla's voice calling my name as I proceeded to hang up the phone.

"Yeah, Kayla, what were you saying?"

"How was Keith and Miami?"

"He was great. It was great." I pressed end on the cordless telephone and dialed another number.

I did not want to admit it, but it was time for the truth to come out. I said out loud, "My name is Chante Chambers, and I am a whore!"

Fifteen

I was a no good, not to be trusted, lying little whore. If I was not making love to Keith, then I was bouncing on Jason's pogo stick. Why? The hell if I knew. I attended some meetings for a nymphomaniac support group. I even joined the damn thing to get some answers. Why was I a whore? Why couldn't I get enough? Why wasn't Keith enough? After about three and a half meetings, I realized that I wasn't a nymphomaniac. I was not addicted to sex. I was addicted to Jason McGee.

So what the hell was my problem? Why did I crave Jason? I had an appointment at two with a psychologist to find out. Jason was going to pay for me to learn how to stop giving him sex. Most sessions were an hour, but I was paying for two hours. I needed one hour to know why I couldn't stop having sex with him and the other hour to learn how to just say no.

"Make yourself comfortable," Dr. Phylicia Blue said, pointing to the tan leather sofa.

She did not have to tell me twice. I took my red heels off and comfortably laid down.

"I like your blouse. Is that Prada?"

My doctor knew her designers. She better know what the hell my problem was since I was about to charge a thousand dollars on my corporate American Express card. I planned on listing the charge on my expense report as research.

"Thank you." I smiled. "A friend of mine likes to buy me things from Prada. Personally, I think Jason is fucking some girl who works for Prada and she gives him discounts." There was no need to keep that comment to myself since I was about to tell the doctor all of my business anyway.

Dr. Blue stopped writing and looked over the rim of her glasses at me in shock. Maybe she didn't think words like that could come out of the mouth of someone who looked as sweet as me. Maybe she was shocked I opened up so soon. Or just maybe she was the Prada connection. I wouldn't be surprised. Jason got around.

"I was prepared to ask you what brings you here today and allow you some time to open up." She brushed that one piece of hair that kept falling in her eye behind her ear and readjusted her glasses. "But based upon what you've said, Jason's the problem?"

"Yes. No. Well he's part of the problem." I sat up. "I can't stop fucking him."

I lay back down.

Once again she looked over her glasses at me. The look on her face screamed this was going to be good. She sipped whatever she had in her coffee mug and wrote something on her notepad. I wanted to ask her what she was drinking and if I could have some.

"You can't stop fucking him," she repeated.

"No, I can't. I just can't." I was finally happy to share my sexcapades with someone who could actually help me. Mecca called me after she received the message I left on her answering machine. She basically told me that the situation I was in wasn't a bad one. She said it was okay. If she weren't in a relationship with Ray, she would probably be sleeping with two or three guys.

I laughed because being in a relationship had never stopped Mecca from sleeping around.

"Is there a reason why you should stop fucking Jason?"

"Well, yes, I'm sorry I didn't explain it clearly. I am in a relationship with Keith and then Jason just happened. Now I am in a relationship with both of them." The thought of Keith made me cry.

Dr. Blue handed me a Kleenex. "I see."

"I love Keith to death. If he ever found out about this, I don't know what I would do. The last thing I want to do is hurt Keith. This is the first real relationship I've had in years. He treats me right. He understands me and does things for me just because. He trusts me." I began to cry again. "I'm not worthy of him or his trust."

"Chante, why do you feel you're not worthy of him or his trust?"

"Because he loves me, and I am giving what should only be between me and him to Jason. Dr. Blue, I prayed for a man like Keith. He's everything I want in a man and more. Yet, I want Jason. "

"Tell me about Jason?"

I began the saga of Chante and Jason.

"...then I met Keith. I met him on Wednesday. We were inseparable until Monday. By Monday afternoon, Jason and I were screwing. It was so damn good!

"After Jason and I had sex in my office, Keith wanted to

have dinner. I wanted to cancel because I felt so guilty. Have you ever slept with a man and had to face another lover that same day?"

"I can relate." She smiled. "But, Chante, this isn't about me. This is about you. So please continue."

"That night, Keith picked me up for our date. He washed me up." I was smiling harder than I needed to be smiling. "My man bathed me. He serenaded me as I dressed. We walked around Central Park. I date high profile men, and they damn sure ain't into that kind of shit. But Keith was different. It didn't matter if he wanted to walk around the park with me or not. I wanted to walk around the park and so he did it.

"He made me dinner. We talked for hours. Men try to fuck me, they don't try to talk any longer than it would take to get my panties down. But Keith was full of conversation. He wanted to know about my childhood.

"I was ready to pull my panties down at the dining room table. Keith didn't have sex in mind. He took me outside to look at the stars and constellations. The next morning, I woke up in his arms with my clothes still on in the same position we looked at the stars in. After that night, I knew Keith was a keeper and I planned on keeping him for as long as I could.

"But now I don't know how much longer I can keep this up." The thought of Keith finding out about Jason brought tears to my eyes once again. Dr. Blue handed me another Kleenex.

"I kept my distance from Jason, after the encounter in my office. I avoided him for a good two months maybe even three. I didn't even miss him. Keith was by my side five days out of the week, if not more. The moment Keith went out of town, here comes Jason.

"He knocked on my door, saying all the things I wanted to and needed to hear years ago. I enjoyed hearing he loved me, he's sorry he hurt me, and he would never do it again. From then on it's been Chante and Jason. Jason and I have been boyfriend and girlfriend since the end of October.

"I've sat on the phone with Keith and told him how much I love him while Jason was showering in my bathroom. I know it was wrong. I flew down to Miami to be with Keith, only to come home and be with Jason." I stood and began to walk around the office.

"Dr. Blue, I need answers." I reached my hands up to the Lord. I needed a blessing from him as well. "Why can't I keep my legs closed? It's not that Keith doesn't satisfy me. He does! Oh, girl, does he." With raised eyebrows, I gave her that, 'he be tearing it up, look.

Dr. Blue flashed me that, 'Girl, I know' grin.

"How is the sex with Jason?"

Why the hell did she want to know that? I guess I was a little too free with my business. Was she trying to help me or was she just being nosy? I hate the fact that Jason makes me insecure. With the mentioning of his name by another female, I immediately get feelings of jealousy and insecurity.

"I'm asking because maybe Keith's sex lacks something that Jason's possesses."

I was glad she cleared that one up.

"Jason's sex is great!" I said great like my name was Tony the Tiger, and I was describing Frosted Flakes. "There's no comparison between the two."

"Why do you say that?"

"Well, Jason fucks me. And Keith makes love to me."

"Do you like to be fucked or would you prefer to be made love to?"

"I would prefer to be made love to and I would love Jason to do it."

Dr. Blue stopped writing and immediately looked up at me and smiled. "You just answered your own question."

"I did?" I asked, confused.

"When you told me the history of Jason and yourself, you told me numerous times that you loved him. You also said the only reason you two broke up was because he repeatedly cheated on you. You said and I quote, Image is everything." She did the fingers thing. "So you didn't break up with Jason because you wanted to. You broke up with him because you cared more about what others would think or say, more so than because you no longer wanted to be with him. So deep down in your heart, you still crave him. Chante, you are still in love with Jason."

Dr. Blue read me like a book. She was telling my life story like the chapter of Jason was sitting on my chest. I sat up on the couch and attentively listened.

"Chante, your problem with Jason is not about sex. You love him. You have sex with Jason, he speaks to you any kind of way and buys you things. That's not what you want, because if so, you would not be with Keith.

"Keith offers you all the things you want in a man, physically, mentally, spiritually, and sexually. But he's not Jason. That's why you stray back to Jason. You have had time to evaluate a relationship with Keith as opposed to Jason. And you aren't willing to give up all that you have with Keith."

I lay back down and closed my eyes as Dr. Blue spoke. Every word she uttered was true. I did love Jason. I had been in love with him since the day I met him. However, it was time for me to accept that Jason was not Keith and would never be. Jason was the man I wanted on the outside and in the bedroom. Keith was the soul I wanted embedded in Jason's body. The whole time, I was sleeping with Keith and Jason, I wasn't dealing with two men, I was trying to create one man: the perfect man for me.

I opened my eyes. "Dr. Blue, how can I stop loving Jason?"

Sixteen

Where the heck was my angel? I searched through all the storage bins that contained the Christmas ornaments and other decorations. Quickly, I surveyed the room and everyone it in. Keia was decorating the tree with pink bulbs. Nicole, her mother, smiled as she hung her stocking from the fireplace. I smiled at her. There was no time to be happy about or think about the power of pussy and its persuasion. I had to find my angel. Keith stopped wrapping the lights around the tree after seeing the look of confusion on my face.

"What's the matter, Baby?" He sat down next to me on the top step and placed his arm around me.

"Have you seen my angel?"

"Where was it?"

Keia looked at us, giggled and continued to hang ornaments on the tree with the assistance of her mother.

"Last year, I wrapped her up and put her in the storage bin right there with my pink glass balls, my Miss Piggy and Kermit The Frog ornament, and the picture of me, my brother, my mother, and my father." I looked through the bin again. "I see everything except the black angel."

Keith wiped my tears as they began to fall from my eyes.

"Baby, you'll find it."

"Keith, my angel isn't lost! Every year I pack it in the same place, and now it's gone. Someone stole my damn angel."

He wiped another tear.

"Don't cry, Chante," Keia said. "My daddy can buy you a new one."

"I saw a beautiful black angel at this store in Harlem on 125ᵗʰ Street." Nicole sat on the other side of me. "I can pick it up for you. It's the least that I can do."

"Christmas is tomorrow," Keith said looking at his daughter's mother with the 'dumb bitch' stare that Nick Lachey gave to Jessica Simpson on *Newlyweds* when she asked him was the tuna fish chicken because the can said chicken of the sea.

"Thanks for the offer, Nicole. But that's okay. That angel has been in my family forever. It was passed down to me when my mother and father moved to Florida. That was my first Christmas without my mother. I had just started writing for the soaps, and couldn't get enough time off to be with my family.

"On Christmas Eve, UPS was at my door. Inside the box was the black angel. She looked so pretty, like my mother cleaned her up just for me. My mother's exact words were 'take care of our angel. You break her you die.'" I chuckled.

"She also said something about not being home for the holidays with the family, but having a part of the family with me for the holidays."

Keith kissed my forehead. "Baby, I don't think someone stole your angel. We'll find it before tomorrow."

Keia giggled again.

What the hell was so funny? Keith must've thought the same thing since he shot Keia a look that shut her up quickly.

"Nicole, can you answer the phone for me," I asked looking through the storage bin again, this time Keith helped.

"That was your doorman, Franklin. He said you had some visitors. I told him to send them up. Was that alright?" Nicole asked, hanging up the telephone.

"Yeah. It's probably Kayla and Shawn or Rita." I stopped looking for the angel and headed to the kitchen to check on dinner and to make a drink.

I needed something to calm my nerves. I wanted a glass of Moet, but I was out. A glass of Hennessy was going to have to do the trick. If Keia and Nicole weren't there, I would have had Keith calm my nerves another way.

"Tae Tae," I heard Kayla's voice.

"I'm in the kitchen."

"Baby, come here." Keith called.

I hurried and gulped down the rest of my brown juice.

"What do you want..." My eyes widened as I walked down the hallway. I blinked just to make sure I was seeing right.

"Mommy!" I rushed into my mother's arms.

"Look who I found in the hallway," Kayla said smiling as she stood next to my brother, his third baby mama, and all four of my nieces.

I hugged and kissed every last one of them, even Tionna, the third baby mama. And I couldn't stand her.

Keith and Keia stood next to me smiling from ear to ear.

"You did this?" I asked.

The twinkle in his eye answered me.

"Merry Christmas," Keia said.

"Thank you." I kissed Keith and Keia.

"Mommy, where's Daddy?" I asked.

My mother cut her eyes at me and proceeded to examine Keith.

"Walter Jr., where is Daddy?" I asked my brother.

My mother answered for him. "You know your father is so goddamn stubborn. He felt like if you wanted to get married, you should get married in front of him." She walked away from me toward the Christmas tree.

"Who is getting married?" I asked, looking around. "Walter Jr., you marrying Tionna?"

"Hell no!" We looked like twins with identical frowns.

She rolled her eyes.

"Well, then who's getting married?" I asked again.

"You are," Keith said.

"There goes the surprise!" Keia rolled her eyes. She went into the den and came back with my black angel.

"Here." She handed Keith the angel.

"Your mother kinda ruined this for me," Keith said, "but the feelings are the same. I love you, baby. Before I actually met you, I knew I was going to spend the rest of my life with you. You are my destiny." He got down on one knee. "Chante Marie Chambers, will you marry me?" He handed me the angel. On top of her halo was more bling bling than any chick could have asked for.

"You better say yes." Kayla's eyes widened at the size of the diamond. "Damn that, you better say Hell Yes!"

I dropped to my knees and almost choked Keith with my tongue.

It took a long minute for me to realize that Keith and I weren't alone. During that minute, I proceeded to pull off my sweater and was beginning to unbutton Keith's shirt. Thank the Lord for tank tops.

"Um hum," Kayla cleared her throat to get our attention.

"Is this what you two do in front of my child?" Nicole said, covering Keia's eyes smiling.

Walter Jr.'s big hands were covering the eyes of his four girls.

"I'm sorry," I said embarrassed. "I forgot where I was."

"I set this all up when I was in Florida, before you came down. I had a talk with your mother and father," Keith said helping me up. "I have his blessing to ask for your hand in marriage although he's not here. When I spoke to him yesterday, he was coming. I don't know what happened between yesterday and today."

We both looked over at my mother and she rolled her eyes.

"So was that a yes?" Keith asked.

"That was a hell yes!" I replied.

Twelve days before Christmas, a gift box arrived at my house or the office each day courtesy of my Daddy. Jason was upset I broke up with him and was trying to woo me back with gifts. I felt compelled to fuck him. I invited him to dinner and made love to him afterwards. We actually made love. After which, I vowed never to do it again. So far I had kept that vow. I returned each one of the gifts on the same day I received it as Dr. Blue advised. *Note: I did not mention our dinner date to her.*

On Christmas day, I received a box containing all of the gifts plus an extra one for Christmas courtesy of my Daddy.

"That was very nice of your father to send you all of that for Christmas." Keith stood over me as I opened the box delivered by an armored guard. "You must be a daddy's girl, like Keia."

Keith smiled and kissed Keia on her forehead.

My mother and brother knew my cheap ass father didn't send that box containing gold and Gucci, platinum and Prada, and of course diamonds.

My mother grabbed my arm and pulled me away from Keith. "Who else are you sleeping with?"

All I could do was shake my head. I noticed my brother staring at me, grinning.

"Playa Playa," he said out loud looking at Tionna. I knew the comment was meant for me.

I stared at my brother with an expressionless face.

Seventeen

Breakfast and lunch poured out of my throat and into the toilet. Every time I tried to pick myself up off the tiled floor, more fluid came flushing out. There I sat in a pair of black slacks with the toilet bowl between my legs and my arms resting on the bowl. Rosemary kept buzzing me for something; I couldn't get up. I had no idea what I had eaten these last few days that had me glued to the toilet. I was confused as to who was the boss and who was the assistant based upon the way Rosemary kept buzzing me.

When it seemed I had the vomiting under control, I held onto the sink and pulled myself up. Listerine swished around in my mouth while I washed my face. As soon as I dried my mouth with the hand towel, more liquid began to pour out of my mouth. I barely made it to the sink. The reflection in the mirror shook its head. *Not now.* I was not up to cleaning throw up out of the sink. I didn't care if it was mine or not.

"This is Chante Chambers. Can you please send housekeeping up to my office?" I found the strength to walk over to my desk and grab the phone.

My next destination was over to the couch. My plan was to lie there until Kayla waddled her behind into my office.

No, this little Hispanic lady didn't just tell me it would be an hour. "No, I can't wait an hour. You need to get someone up here now." The receiver went crashing into the cradle.

As I made my way over to the couch, I decided to see what was so important that had Rosemary buzzing me like she was retarded. After unlocking my door and opening it, I rolled my eyes at the sight of Rosemary doing her usual, talking on the phone. Why had I expected her to be working?

"Uh Um." I cleared my throat to let her know I was standing there.

She swiveled around in her chair, never once putting the phone down. "Yes, Chante?"

"What the hell did you want?" I had a lot of attitude. I was PMSing big time.

"Excuse me?" Rosemary replied in shock.

Bitch, did I stutter? "What the hell did you want? You were buzzing me like a bat out of hell. Evidently you forgot that you were my assistant since you keep buzzing me as if I was going to walk out here to you."

What I just said didn't make much sense given the fact that I did just walk out to her. Her facial expression told me that. Duh!

Rosemary rolled her eyes at me. "Well, your boss was down here. Since your door was locked, he couldn't get in. So I buzzed you repeatedly at his request."

She took pride in saying 'your boss was here so, I buzzed you repeatedly at his request.' I swear if she didn't do good work, her ass would have been fired a long time ago. Once again I felt like an ass. However, common sense should have told her that when I didn't answer the first time to let it go.

"Jason said for you to come upstairs." She resumed her phone conversation.

"Tell Jason I will see him when I see him," I said as I slammed my door shut.

I had done everything Dr. Blue had said concerning distancing myself from Jason. Except, I had no intentions of distancing myself from Jason. He was my boss and I was not leaving my nice cushy set up. However, I did plan to keep the shit strictly professional at all times. Dr. Blue was worth every penny Jason was paying her.

The buzzing began again. What did Rosemary want now? I had no energy to get up, walk over to my desk, and respond to the buzzing intercom. I reached up from the couch and turned the doorknob.

In walked Kayla. My pregnant friend was in diva mode.

"Chante, get ya ass up before you make me late for my appointment."

I sat up to make room for Kayla to sit down on the couch.

"That's cute." I referred to her outfit.

She stood up and modeled. "You like?"

"You better stop before your butt tips over." We laughed.

"Well, once Keith puts some babies up in there, you, too, will look as fabulous as me in your Gucci." She tickled my stomach.

The gagging in my throat began again, and I rushed to the nearest trashcan. After about five minutes of worshiping the garbage, Kayla handed me a towel. She looked at me puzzled. Then she smiled.

"Chante, are you pregnant?"

"No," I said firmly.

"Yes, you are."

"No, I am not. I ate something that just didn't agree with my stomach." I omitted the fact that I had been throwing up for the last few weeks and I was late. I told her the same lie I told Keith.

"Okay, whatever," Kayla said taking my winter white cashmere coat from the closet.

♫

"Do you see that right there?" Dr. Cynthia Woodson asked as she rolled the probe over Kayla's belly. "That's the baby's vagina."

"Oh my God! Oh my God! It's a girl. You hear that, Tae Tae, you have a goddaughter." Kayla was excited. "Shawn is going to be disappointed since he wanted a boy. Oh well, it's another girl for him."

The mentioning of Shawn's name made me want to vomit. I managed to contain myself. I didn't know how he managed to make his way back into the house, but he had. Kayla hadn't shared that with me. Shawn was not my headache he was hers. One thing for sure, I didn't want to hear about his cheating again.

Dr. Woodson rolled the probe over Kayla's stomach a little more with a complex look on her face.

"I wasn't prepared for this," she mumbled. She then glanced at Kayla's chart.

"Is something wrong?" Kayla asked with tears forming.

"Remember last time when we listened to the baby's heartbeat, and I thought it was a little abnormal? Like it was beating too fast." Dr. Woodson picked the probe back up and resumed the ultrasound.

"Yes," Kayla began to cry.

"I just figured out why that was. Do you see that right there?" Dr. Woodson pointed to the monitor with her free hand. "That's your son's penis."

Kayla looked at Dr. Woodson with that 'whatcha talking about, Willis' face. "Excuse me?"

"The heartbeat sounded fast, abnormal for a fetus. And that was because we were hearing both heartbeats. One baby was in front of the other." She pointed to the screen again. "That there is your son's penis," the doctor repeated.

"I have two babies growing inside me?" Kayla asked.

I felt like saying you know good and well in these short months your fat ass did not blow up like that over one bigheaded baby. That day in Carol's Café she looked like she had put on a good ten to fifteen pounds.

"Kayla, for how long have I been telling you it was twins? Stop acting like it couldn't happen to you," I said, "like twins don't run in your family. Isn't your mother a twin? I kept telling you it was more than one bigheaded baby in there."

I smiled. I was happy for her. As Dr. Woodson continued to exam Kayla, I sat in the black leather chair and looked around the room. An entire wall was full of pictures of babies that she had delivered over the years. On the back of the door hung a diagram of a woman's reproductive organs, a diagram of different birth control pills and a diagram of a pregnant woman. For one brief moment thoughts of being a mommy danced in my head. I looked down at my bloated abdomen, and shook my head.

"Okay Kayla, I'll see you again in four weeks," Dr. Woodson said as she exited the room.

I followed her out. "Dr. Woodson can I make an appointment to see you?"

Eighteen

I patiently waited for the one line to appear on my home pregnancy test. Dr. Woodson did not know what the hell she was talking about when she said I was almost five weeks pregnant. Her test was wrong! They were all wrong! The EPT I had taken the night before, the Fact Plus I used before this Clear Blue Easy, were all defected. How in the hell could I be pregnant? *Easy, damn it! When was the last time you used a condom?*

I could not have this baby. Who in the hell was the daddy? Jason or Keith? I was not going to be one of those girls on Maury, arguing with some man, his mama, and his new girlfriend claiming he was my baby's daddy.

I closed my eyes, said a quick prayer, and crossed my fingers. Despite my prayer, I was pregnant. There was no way I could have this baby. I was marrying Keith. How could I pass a little chocolate baby off as Keith's?

According to Dr. Woodson's calculation the baby was conceived in December. Jason and I had had sex a few times in December. I replayed a few sex sessions in my mind with both Keith and Jason, and I knew Jason was the father.

This baby was conceived when I took Jason to dinner. I knew I should've gotten off of him, but no, I lay on top of him and allowed his juices to marinate. What in the hell was

I going to do?

I loved Keith with all my heart. What was I going to say to him, 'Baby, I love you. By the way, I cheated on you. Now I'm pregnant, and Jason's the father. I want you to accept that and still marry me.' Hell no! Keith wasn't going to find out about this. I threw the pregnancy test into the garbage and prepared for work.

♫

"Chante, hold that elevator," Jason screamed, coming toward the closing doors.

"Okay." I smiled and pressed the close door button.

"You're pressing the wrong button," a blond haired, blue-eyed black girl said as she stuck her arm out in the path of the closing doors.

"Thanks." Jackass. Who in the hell said I wanted to be in an elevator with Jason. I was avoiding him at all costs. I must admit it; February was almost over and I was doing well.

The blond haired blue-eyed floozy got off the elevator on the tenth floor, which left Jason and I alone. The last thing I wanted was to be alone with Jason. Damn sure not for a ride up twenty-six flights. I was not strong enough yet. My main purpose for avoiding him was I could not guarantee that my panties would not come down or make their way over to the side. I looked him over. He looked good. Smelled good. He was smiling at me.

"Why have you been avoiding Daddy?"

"Jason, leave me alone." I stood in my corner of the elevator. My eyes never looked in his direction.

"Did you enjoy your twelve days of Christmas?"

"I gave it away," I mumbled.

"Why did you do that?" He came closer.

"Didn't want it." I slid over.

"Looks like you kept one thing." Jason pushed my hair behind my ear to admire the diamond earring I was wearing. "On Christmas, I came by your place. Franklin said you weren't there."

"I wasn't." I kept a few of the gifts. I gave my mother a beautiful cashmere wrap, Kayla a necklace with a charm, and Keia a pair of diamond studs. The rest I kept.

"I tried to spend New Year's Eve with you." He massaged my neck. "Bought tickets to the Black and White Ball. Them shits cost me a grip."

"Did they really?" I removed his hand.

Jason caught a good view of the rock gracing my ring finger.

"Oh, this is why you haven't been returning my calls. Or why I haven't really seen you since that night at the hotel. This also explains why you sent my shit back and why you weren't home on Christmas. You're about to marry some dude? You wearing my mother fucking earrings, yet you're rocking his ring. Who is he?"

"Jason, does it matter who he is?" I faced him. "You're not going to marry me. You're not going to give me what I need in a man." I would have given up all of my platinum, Prada, and Keith if he said he would.

Jason trapped me in the elevator by pulling the stop button. I was slightly frightened. I balled my fist up and clutched my bag with my other hand. If he wanted a fight, I was going to beat his ass with the Dior bag Kayla bought me for Christmas. In between swinging this bag, punches would be thrown. Better yet, I could do more damage if I took my boots off and hit him with the heel. Steadily, I watched him to see his next move.

Why didn't I mush his head away? I couldn't. Why didn't I move away? I was frozen. Why didn't I say no, stop, Jason? I was mute. Why had I given the palace guard the day off? I had a lunch date with Keith. I had no intention of riding Daddy's dick. I was not going to do it. Instead, I was going to just stand there and continue to let Jason eat me. My head rolled back in pleasure. My brown suede riding boot, took one step back, allowing me to raise my dress up to my waist.

From somewhere, I was blessed with strength. Enough strength to push Jason's head deeper into the palace. His hands grasped my bare ass pulling me into him. Just like that both of my thick brown thighs were around Jason's neck. He braced himself, never once removing his tongue, to stand up. His tongue continued to flicker over the palace's doorbell, as all my weight rested on his shoulders.

The elevator resumed moving. After I wiped the cream off of my thighs, I handed Jason a handkerchief to wipe his mouth. Jason looked at me and smiled. I tried not to look his way.

He knew he was the man after I yelled out, "This is just so good!"

Still staring at me, he grinned. "Can that nigga do that as well as I just did?"

Shocked was the expression on my face. Jason was an

asshole. There were always motives behind everything he did. He couldn't just lick the twat because he was craving it; instead, he wanted to compare. He wanted to brag about his tongue action. I was not going to give him the satisfaction.

"He's better." I winked. "I don't yell out this is just so good to him. For my man I yell out this shit is great!"

I was so happy we were approaching the thirty-sixth floor. I could no longer stomach Jason. I waited for the elevator doors to open, stepped off the elevator, and turned to face him.

"Jason, I'm pregnant."

Jason's bottom lip hit the floor. Rosemary caught a glimpse of his facial expression and diverted all of her attention to him.

"What?" Jason called out as the elevator doors closed in his face.

♫

"How do I know the baby's mine?" Jason asked as he walked into my office and shut the door.

I gave Jason the 'don't go there' look.

"If it wasn't yours, do you think I would waste my time telling you?"

"You fucking some other dude." Jason caught my 'don't go there' look again. "I'm sorry."

He walked around my desk and stood next to me. "I'll give you money for an abortion."

Money for an abortion? I have health insurance. What the hell made Jason think I wanted to get an abortion? Did I tell him that? Who the hell was he to assume that I wanted an abortion? I mean I did. But what gave him the right to make that decision for me?

"I know a place you can go to that's very discreet," Jason continued to speak.

Did he not see the look on my face? Did he not see this bitch was steaming? Could he not detect that if he didn't get the hell away from me quickly that I was going to knock him the fuck out?

"Jason. Jason. JASON!" He really needed to shut up. "Let's backtrack for one minute. Did I say I wanted to abort your baby?"

"No, but you're marrying dude, remember?"

"Jason that was a rhetorical question it was not meant for you to answer. I do not plan on having our baby. However, what the hell gives you the right to make the choice of an abortion for me? Who the hell told you to even bring it up?

"Then you come at me like I am one of your whores. I thought I was bigger than your average whore. I thought I was special. I'm the one that gets all the Prada, Marc Jacobs, Dolce & Gabbana, Jimmy Choos, and Manolos that your money can buy. You love me.

"Remember when you told me that? You love me so much. You will never hurt me again. Please, Chante, let's try this again. You miss me. You missed eating my pussy. That's all you missed. Because if you loved me the way you claimed, when you saw the rock on my finger, you wouldn't have eaten the shit out of my ass to compare licks to the next man.

"And when I told you I had your child in my womb, you would've been making plans for us to be a family. But immediately you bring up abortion. Instead of picking out wedding gowns, china patterns, baby furniture, baby clothes and etcetera, you want to send me to the clinic. The same clinic you send the rest of your whores."

I searched Jason's face for some indication that my words had an effect on him. I wanted him to say, Chante, I meant every word I said to you. I want you. I want our baby. His face showed no feelings.

"Tae Tae." He wiped my tears.

Please tell me you love me.

"You broke up with me, remember?" he said. "I didn't break up with you. I meant what I said when I came to your house that night. I was prepared to do right by you or at least try. And I think I was doing a good job.

"I'm sitting there chilling with you and dude calls. You sexing me talking to this nigga on the phone telling him how much you love him. How the fuck you think that made me feel? I'm a man, and although I didn't say anything, I still have feelings."

"Jason, I would give up all I have just to be happy with you."

He chuckled. "Then you lie to me and tell me you went to Miami with Kayla. I know you were there with dude. But I didn't say nothing. I figured I did you wrong in the past so you was just getting payback or some stupid shit like that."

I cried harder. I loved Keith to death. However I loved Jason more than I loved myself. I was willing to give Keith up and forever remain faithful to Jason if he could promise me everything I have in Keith.

"Jason, I love you."

"You seem to be happier with dude. Go ahead marry him. Let him take care of your baby." He opened the door and closed it behind him.

♫

"Chante, Chante," Keith called from the bathroom.

I was relaxing on the chaise in my bedroom, reading a book. I was in no rush to see what Keith wanted. If he had truly wanted me, he knew where to find me.

"Chante," Keith continued to call me.

I hung off the chaise, to look at Keith in the bathroom. "Yes baby."

"Come here."

"Keith, do I have to?" I whined. "I'm comfortable. Plus this book is getting good."

"Bring your lazy butt in here." He grinned at me. "I'll carry you back to your spot, you couch potato."

"What do you want, baby?" I asked as I stood next to Keith at the his and her sinks.

Keith reached into the garbage can. Smiling, he revealed six used pregnancy tests, all containing the same results.

"Am I going to be a daddy?"

Shit. Why hadn't I taken the garbage out? What could I say? I couldn't say no. The word pregnant was spelled out on one of the tests.

"Yes, I am pregnant." *However it's not your baby.* The thought made me recap this morning's conversation with Jason. It triggered tears.

"Don't cry, Baby." He wiped my tears. "This is a happy time. I'm happy."

Why couldn't the father show the same excitement?

Keith picked me up and spun me around. As soon as he placed my feet back on the floor, I pulled my nightshirt down since my entire ass was hanging out.

He bit his bottom lip and grinned. "Nah, Baby, take that off."

Sex was the last thing I wanted. It was the farthest thing from my mind. I was still dealing with the love of my life telling me to marry someone else and let him take care of *my* baby.

"Keith, I really don't feel like it," I looked at him with pleading eyes.

"Please take the shirt off." He kissed my forehead.

My gown dropped to the floor. Keith took a few steps back and admired my naked body.

"Where you going?" I asked as Keith walked out of the bathroom.

"I'll be back, just wait right there."

Keith returned to the bathroom with my digital camera in one hand and a tripod in the other.

"Oh, no, I don't do cameras and the butt naked thing."

"Chante, I am not trying to submit ya pictures to Playboy." Keith laughed and adjusted the picture.

After that whole Derrick incident, I didn't play that naked pictures crap. However, I trusted Keith. I swear to God if those pictures made it on to anybody's website or somebody's magazine, I would be facing a murder charge, more realistically my brother would have another assault charge.

I posed. "So are you saying I'm not good enough for

Playboy?"

"Come on, Ma. You did your thing in *Vixen*. You're definitely hot. You are more voluptuous than Beyoncé." He smiled. "You got an apple bottom and nice big succulent breast, plus a cute face."

I patiently stayed still in my sexy girl pose.

"Take your arm and cover your breast. I know that's hard because they are so big and succulent, but you make that happen," He laughed as he posed me. "Now somehow cover your crotch and hold your stomach."

"What?" I was two seconds from saying fuck this picture and sitting back down.

"Here put these panties on," He handed me some pink lace panties. "Now accent your stomach. Each month I am going to do this to you and watch your sexy ass get fat."

He took the picture.

"It doesn't matter how fat you get, you'll always be my sexy fat mama. I'm not just saying that because you are about to have my son either." He took another picture.

I did as Keith asked. On the outside I was smiling. Inside I was crying. Keith would never see the birth of this baby. He was not supposed to know it existed.

The man was taking pictures of a non-existent stomach. He planned to document the growth of my belly. Keith was looking forward to being a daddy for the second time. There was no way I would carry this baby for nine months and pass it off as his, as Jason suggested. The thought crossed my mind, yet it wouldn't be right. I was going along with the abortion as planned.

Keith placed the camera on the tripod and pressed some

buttons. As the timer went off, a picture was captured. Keith kissed my stomach as a tear fell from my eye.

Nineteen

"Congratulations," Dr. Blue said at the first glance of my swollen abdomen. She held her office door open for me.

I ignored her and walked in.

"I guess you and Keith are doing well. That would explain the gut and me not seeing you in what three or four months." She smiled.

"More like closer to five months," I mumbled.

My trench coat never made it to the coat rack, as intended. I hadn't had the strength to pick it up. As I leaned against the wall to take my green Gucci loafers off, I felt Dr. Blue give me a look over. From my bare feet to my designer jeans up to my green shirt, she sized me up. Her smiled vanished with a quick glance at my facial expression.

"I messed up." I threw up my hands. I walked over to the sofa and assumed the position.

She sipped whatever she had in that coffee mug. I believed it to be some type of liquor. There was no way she could listen to a bunch of wealthy, spoiled nuts all day and not take a drink. If she didn't drink at work, she damn sure had to hit the bottle hard at home. She took a minute or two to observe me, and figure out the best approach.

With her pointer finger, she pushed her glasses up on her face and began our session. "How did you mess up, Chante?"

"Just as I had my life figured all out, as soon as I got to my comfort zone, to a time and place where I was happy, something comes along and fucks it all up." I paused and allowed myself a moment to just let my mind wander.

"I did everything you said regarding Jason. I must admit in the beginning it was hard. I slipped up a time or two." I closed my eyes and grinned. "It was more like three or four times. But anyway. I broke off whatever it was that Jason and I called ourselves having.

"I returned the diamond trinkets from my twelve days of Christmas, as you advised. But he only gave them back. Despite all you said about accepting gifts from Jason, I gladly accepted. My mother always said if something were meant to be, it would come back to you. So I figured since they came back, it was meant for me to have them. I gave away a few things, yet I kept most of it. Jason has great taste.

"I haven't been here in months because at first I thought I was cured. I was making progress. Keith proposed, I accepted. Life was good. And then I found out I was pregnant."

"Why is being pregnant a bad thing? Eventually you and Keith were going to start a family, right?

"Dr. Blue, I am carrying Jason's baby." I busted out crying.

Her left eyebrow rose in shock. She passed me a Kleenex, then wrote on her notepad, and continued to listen.

"I told him I was pregnant. I told Jason I would give up

all that I have including Keith to have happiness with him. And you know what he had a nerve to say? He threw it up in my face that this time he wanted our love thing to work.

"He was sincere. He was trying to do right by me. I broke up with him. I lied to him. I sat on the phone with another man while he and I was sexing. I went to Miami to be with a man, and he knew this. He said he figured I was getting payback for all he had done to me in the past. And that was cool. He could forgive me for that. But I broke up with him. I broke his heart. I hurt him."

I blew my nose. "I told Jason I was sorry and I wanted him. That bastard looked me in my eyes and told me that I was happier with Keith, go ahead marry him and let him take care of my baby."

"Chante, I am so sorry to hear that."

"Don't be. I fucked up. I fucked up a good thing with Keith. I was willing to give him up just to be with Jason."

"So what does Keith say about it all?"

"Keith says nothing because Keith knows nothing." I sat up quickly.

"So does he think you have just gained a few pounds?"

"Keith knows I'm pregnant. He thinks it's his." My voice trailed off.

"Chante, that's not healthy. If you are not honest with Keith now, when will the lies stop? You can't let Keith continue to believe that."

"You think I don't know that?" I raised my voice. "Why the fuck do you think I am here? If I were going to pass the baby off as Keith's, there would be no need for my tears or my visit to you. I must admit that lately I have not been acting like the child my mother raised, but I am not a horrible person that would have a baby by one man and allow another man to think it was his, knowing it wasn't."

I grabbed my wristlet from the coffee table and stood up. "What kind of woman do you take me for?"

"Chante, I apologize if I offended you. That was not my intention."

I continued to put my shoes back on.

"Chante, we still have about thirty minutes left in the session. Let's continue to talk. We can come up with solutions for telling Keith." Dr. Blue was sincere.

"I can't. I have an appointment that I need to keep," I said, closing the door behind me.

Twenty

Concentrating on the bright lights, I stared at the ceiling. Occasionally my eyes wandered around at the collage of pictures all over the four walls of the small room. The light sounds of Maxwell filled the room, yet it didn't hide the suctioning sound. My legs shook as my feet rested in the stirrups. How women could repeatedly abort babies was beyond me. After this I would never do it again.

As I lay on the table, so many thoughts entered my mind. The number one thought was what in the hell was I going to tell Keith? I carried this baby for as long as I could. For weeks, I allowed Keith to take my picture naked, kiss my baby goodnight, and a host of other things. As my stomach began to bulge, entering the third month of pregnancy, he had heard the baby's heartbeat. Yesterday, I became five months pregnant. Once again, I undressed and allowed Keith to take a picture. This time I actually had something to hold. The picture captured all of the things it always did, except my smile.

How trifling was I? Here I was going to the doctor every month like I was going to be a mommy. Ever so often Dr. Woodson would look up from her work and cut her eyes at me. If I could tell her the truth, I would tell her I had no intentions of wasting her time and my money by going to prenatal visits, for a pregnancy I wasn't going to see through. The prenatal visits were Keith's idea. The abortion was mine.

I wished I could've explained to her that I was a whore and was carrying another man's baby. I wanted my baby. I loved my baby. Most importantly I wanted Keith to be happy. I wanted this to be his baby. However, the dates didn't match. It was Jason's sperm that fertilized my egg. I could not carry this baby for another four months, deliver the baby, allow Keith to love it, raise it and refer to it as his son or daughter only to crush his heart later.

As soon as Keith announced he was going to LA, I was on the phone scheduling my surgery. By the time his flight landed in LA, it would all be over. The last thing I wanted to do was hurt the man I loved. I knew he was looking forward to the birth of his son. At our last prenatal visit, he questioned when we would know the sex.

"Keith, baby, I am so sorry," I mumbled.

"What was that?" Dr. Woodson asked applying pressure to my abdomen.

"Nothing," I said fighting the pain from her pressure.

I was on the table, legs spread open, feet still in the stirrups as she went over the aftercare instructions. As she talked, I cried. I cried like a baby. What had I just done?

"No, Chante, don't try to get up." She handed me some tissue. "Just relax. I'll be back in about forty-five minutes to an hour. Just relax." She picked up my chart and flipped through it.

"Chante, can I ask you a question?" Dr. Woodson bit her bottom lip.

I was in no mood to have a conversation with anyone. I just wanted to be left alone. I couldn't speak. My eyes answered her.

"Chante, I have known you for too long. I have watched you and Keith come in here faithfully for the last few months. You know he was excited. Why did you do this? I'm asking you this now, as opposed to before the procedure because I didn't want my words to influence your decision."

"It's a long story." I couldn't look her in her eyes.

She dimmed the lights and left the room.

I didn't know what made me think I could drive myself home. I pulled over twice and threw up. The abortion was not making me vomit it was guilt. It should have taken me five minutes to get home, ten minutes max. Yet, here I was an hour after leaving Dr. Woodson's office, pulled over on the side of the road trembling and crying. I was told to bring someone to drive me home. Who was I going to ask? I should've called Jason's ass. Fuck Jason! We hadn't spoken since that day I told him I was pregnant. That told me how sincere he really was.

Slowly, cars drove past me and looked my way as I pounded my car horn with my fist like a mad woman. A motorist actually stopped to ask if I was okay after he witnessed me pouring my guts out onto the curb. I just held onto the motorist and as he held me I cried on his shoulder. That was the first time I had ever found comfort in a white man. I was truly grateful and blessed that he did not rape me, rob me, or kill me. Instead, he called my best friend to come and get me.

His BMW remained behind my Bentley until Kayla's BMW pulled up.

"Chante, open the door." Kayla banged on my window.

"Kayla, I am so sorry. I'm sorry. Tell Keith I am sorry," I cried as snot ran out my nose. She held me in her arms.

"Chante, what happened? What are you sorry for?"

"Just tell Keith I'm sorry." I pushed her away.

Kayla rested her arms on her very pregnant stomach. She looked me up and down in attempt to read me. She couldn't get past the tears. She took some tissue from her coat pocket and wiped my face.

"Is the baby alright?" She questioned.

"The baby is gone." I fell to the ground. "Tell Keith I'm sorry."

Kayla stared at me like drama was the last thing she needed. She had never seen me this distraught. She began to cry.

"You lost the baby?"

My only response was tears. She picked me up off the ground and helped me get into the car. She pulled out her cell phone and a made a call.

♫

Kayla walked into my bedroom with the telephone in her hand. She handed it to me.

"Kayla, I don't want to speak to anyone." I turned my back to her and continued to lie in a ball.

"It's Keith." Once again she handed me the phone.

"Did you tell him I was sorry?" I wiped my eyes as I

turned toward her.

"It's not my place to tell him." She stroked the hair out of my face. "Chante, it's not your fault you lost the baby. Stop acting like it is."

"It is my fault."

"It's not your damn fault, and if you say it is one more time I am going to tell Shawn not to go and get your shrimp scampi and lobster."

I smiled. Kayla knew I loved shrimp and lobster. Shawn was driving to City Island to get us some seafood.

"You and Keith can always have another baby." She smiled. "And as much as y'all do it, that baby will be here in no time."

"Shut up." I half smiled.

"Now talk to your man." She handed me the phone and walked out of the room.

I knew what to say to Keith. Kayla assumed I had a miscarriage, so I just went along with it. I knew it was wrong, misleading, and deceitful, but I didn't want to lose Keith. I did not want him to leave me.

"Hello." My voice was very groggy.

"Hey, Beautiful. " Keith's voice brought tears to my eyes. "Did I wake you?"

"No, I wasn't asleep."

"Why are you crying?"

My sobs were the only sound Keith heard. My cries were real. They were genuine. I was so sorry. If I could kill myself at that moment, I would have.

"I'm sorry, Keith. I am so sorry. Please know that I would never do anything to intentionally hurt you. Baby, I love you."

"Chante, what's wrong?"

"Keith the baby's gone." As I cried, snot ran out of my nose. I tried my best to suck it back up.

Silence.

"Baby, did you hear me?"

"What?"

"Keith the baby is gone,"

I heard Keith cry for the first time.

"You lost our baby?"

"Keith, I am so sorry, baby."

"We lost our baby?"

"Baby, I'm so sorry."

"Chante, it's not your fault. Don't blame yourself. I'm sorry you had to go through this by yourself. Damn it. Something told me not to come to LA."

"Keith, there was nothing you could have done to prevent this." That was the honest to God truth.

"I'll be home tonight. If not, in the morning."

"Keith, I'm sorry, baby. Please don't cut your trip short," I cried. I felt so damn guilty. I felt like shit. Here I was the guilty party and everyone was comforting me. Telling me not to blame myself. I was to blame. I was so overwhelmed with tears I could no longer speak.

"Chante? Chante? Chante, are you still there?"

"I'm here. Keith, I am so sorry. Baby, I am sorry."

"It's okay. I love you. I'm coming home." Keith hung up the phone.

Twenty One

Keith sat in the den bopping his head to music. I couldn't concentrate on the book that I was reading because every twenty seconds or so he would press the right arrow on the stereo remote and the song would change.

"Baby, please stop?" I asked, repositioning my head on his lap.

"Stop what?" He snatched my book out of my hands.

"Come on, baby, stop, this book is getting good." I took my book back.

Once again he snatched the book. "Stop what?"

"Can you allow a song to play out? You keep skipping the song as soon as it begins."

"I'm trying to see if these songs are going to make the cut for Tyra's new album."

"Who the hell is Tyra?"

"The new artist I've been telling you about. You don't remember?"

I looked at Keith with a blank stare.

"That means you don't listen to shit I say."

That wasn't true. I listened to everything Keith said. I loved to hear him speak, yet when he started talking work, I tuned him out. I didn't discuss my work with him either. Work was just that, something to leave at work.

"Now you know that isn't true. What does that have to do with you not allowing the song to play out?"

"I liked how you changed the subject." He kissed my forehead. "If a song doesn't move me in say the first twenty or thirty seconds, it's a wrap."

My expression showed I wasn't amused or interested.

"If I'm bothering you, go in the living room or go in the bedroom."

Keith looked relieved at the sound of the ringing phone. He knew I was about to rip him a new one.

"Excuse me?" I sat up.

He handed me the phone. "Chante, just answer the phone."

"Hello?"

"You have a collect call from Kayla, press one to accept the charges," an operator said.

Quickly I pressed one. Did I hear the operator correctly? Did she say I had a collect call from Kayla? What the hell was Kayla doing calling me collect.

"Kayla, where are you? And why are you calling me collect?"

"Chante, would you shut up!" Kayla's voice was full of attitude. "Just come and get me."

"First answer my question, where are you?"

"Chante, I don't have time for questions. Just come get me from jail and bring $500."

"Okay. I'm on my way."

Keith didn't notice my expression.

"Good, you're leaving. Go do your girl thing with Kayla." He smiled, kicked his legs up on the couch, and skipped to the next song.

"I'm not going to do my girl thing with Kayla. I'm going to bail my best friend out of jail."

"Jail?"

I smiled at the sight of Kayla leaving the police department. After I paid her bail, I waited for her in the car. I had been sitting in my car for over an hour. A sistah was tired. I became even more impatient waiting for Kayla to waddle her ass up to the car.

I smiled as she adjusted her seatbelt around her overdue pregnant belly.

"What the hell are you smiling at?" She snapped.

"You. Since when did pretty girls get locked up?" I laughed.

Kayla shook her head, took a deep breath, made a fist, and bit down on her bottom lip.

"Not right now, Tae Tae."

We drove in silence.

"You were right." She broke the silence.

"Right about what?"

"I called you this morning to go shopping, but Keith said you were sleep. And with everything that you been through this week, it wasn't that important to have him wake you up. So, I asked Shawn to go with me, but he said he had papers to grade.

"So I got cute and went to the mall by myself. Look at my goddamn ankles. They are all swollen and shit from me walking around the mall." She pulled up her pant leg for me to see. Then she began to massage her ankles. "I thought all the walking would make me go into labor. But anyway, here I am walking around the mall buying things for the twins."

"Kayla, what does all of this have to do with me picking you up from jail?" I asked.

No, that heifer did not just roll her eyes at me and huff.

She took a deep breath and exhaled.

"As I was saying, I went shopping. Came home all excited. I couldn't wait to show someone the stuff I brought. I go into Simone's room. She's not there. But her car is in the driveway."

"Car? When did she get a car?" The last I heard Simone was catching the bus.

"She has a red Mercedes. She's had it about a month or two."

"Who did she have to fuck to get a car?"

"Jason. But anyway. Since I couldn't find her, I started looking for Shawn. He's not into the whole baby clothes being cute thing. But what the hell, I was excited, and he was just going to act like he was, too. So I go into the den. He should have been in there grading papers, but I know he's watching ESPN. That bitch was on her knees sucking him off."

My eyes stretched as wide as my sockets would allow as my bottom lip practically hit the steering wheel.

"What?"

"That bitch was on her knees, butt naked sucking Shawn's dick."

"What bitch?" I had to pull over to contain myself. "Are you talking about the same bitch that called the house?"

"No, but ain't no telling if she stopped by prior to Simone giving him a blow job."

Simone.

"I know I shouldn't have hit her, but I allowed that nasty ass bitch to stay in my home, and she pays me back by sucking my man's dick. Oh, hell no. I waddled my ass back down the stairs, to the garage. I think I picked up a wrench or something and commenced to breaking every fucking window on that damn car. Simone came outside. She loves that car. It's the only thing she really owns that's worth something. And I knew it. That's why I did it."

We sat in silence for about a minute, during which I glanced over and saw Kayla with her fists balled up. She exhaled and then exhaled again.

"She came outside, and started cursing at me. Chante, I did something I should have done a long time ago to Tasha. I smacked the shit out of her. And then I smacked her again and again. You know Mrs. Washington, from across the street?"

I nodded yes.

"Well, she called the police. I thought she liked me. But that ole bag called the cops on me. They weren't going to arrest me when they saw that I was pregnant. But then Simone told me that if you and me knew how to please our men they wouldn't come to her to suck their dicks."

No she didn't.

Kayla nodded her head like she knew exactly what I was thinking.

"Chante, when she made that comment. I saw every woman that Shawn had ever cheated with that I knew of, and one face stood out, Tasha's. That bitch said the same exact words to me right before she had a baby with my man. Tae Tae, I lost it. I swung past the cop and punched her dead smack in the mouth."

I smiled. That was my girl.

"Tae Tae, you told me not to trust her. And even after we saw her giving Jason head, I still let her stay in my home." She took another deep breath. "I shouldn't have let Shawn come back. But no, I think with my heart and not my brain."

Kayla handed me my ringing cell phone.

"Look in the glove compartment and pass me my Bluetooth."

"Here." She handed me the earpiece and I answered the phone.

"Yeah," I said after noticing Kayla's home phone number on the Caller ID. "Hello. Hello. Hel-loooooo."

No one spoke directly into the phone. I could make out heavy breathing in between screaming, cursing, crying, and arguing.

"Hel-lo, Shawn, I do not have time for bullshit." I was becoming annoyed.

"This is not Shawn."

"Well, who the hell is this and why are you calling me?"

"Chante, it's me, Simone."

"And what do you want?" Ever since that day I caught her with Jason, I hadn't had too much to say to her. And what was this about Jason buying her a car? I was no longer into Jason, yet I was a little jealous. I was supposed to be the only woman he purchased a car for. At least he bought me a Bentley. Now after this episode with Kayla going to jail because of her, I really had nothing to say to her. I was two seconds from hanging up on the broad. I would not be wasting any daytime minutes on her funky behind.

"Look, I just called to tell you Kayla is in jail. Since you are her friend, maybe you can go get her."

"I have my friend already and by the time I get to her house, you and your shit better be gone. If not, your head will not be the only thing hurting."

"Chante. Chante." I heard Simone calling my name as I proceed to end the call.

"What?" I answered.

"Would you happen to know what Jason's new cell phone number is?" She giggled.

I ended the call.

Once again Kayla clutched her fist. She inhaled deeply, held it and then exhaled.

"What did she want?" Kayla asked through clenched teeth.

"For me to come get you from jail. You heard what I told her, right?"

Kayla said nothing.

"I told her when we get there, she better be gone. If not I'm going to put my foot in her ass. Kayla, I mean this. This is the last time I am going to confront one of Shawn's women for you. I hope you truly learn from this experience. If not, I am still going to be your friend. And I will always love you. I will be the ear you speak into and that shoulder to cry on. But I am not going to anybody else's house, nor am I fighting anyone else or listening to phone calls. Do you understand?"

I looked over at Kayla. Kayla's top lip and teeth were wrapped around her bottom lip. Her nose was scrunched up. Her eyes were closed. Both of her hands were balled up in a fist as tight as they could get. Slowly she rocked back and forth. She shook her head yes.

"What is wrong with you?"

"Take me to the hospital. My water just broke."

Not in the Bentley.

Twenty Two

"I don't know why you and Keith can't wait until the twins are walking so they can be in the wedding."

"Kayla, you must be crazy if you think I am going to plan my wedding around the growth of your rugrats."

"Was that a nice thing to say about your god children?" Kayla asked as we browsed through bridal magazines.

"I could've said much worst. Did you forget that Little Shawn pissed on me?" I rolled my eyes. "And Shana spit up on my white sofa."

Kayla laughed. It was because of Shana's inability to digest her breast milk, which caused us to exit the living room.

"Don't you want a nice spring or summer wedding? We could wear pastels. You know I look good in yellow or soft pink. Imagine an outdoor ceremony. Shana would look so cute in a white fluffy dress dropping rose petals. Everyone would ooh and ah because she is so cute. And you know my little man would look cute in a tux, carrying the ring on a pillow. Can you believe they make tuxedos that small?"

Her smile vanished when she realized I was not budging on my decision.

"Tae Tae, is four or five months going to kill your festivities? What's the big difference between getting married in December as opposed to May or June? The twins will be a year old."

"Kayla, I am getting married on New Year's Eve. I am not changing that for anybody. At exactly twelve o'clock, I will be kissing my husband. Ain't that right, baby?" I walked over to the door since I heard Keith in the hallway.

"Is what right?" he asked sticking his head in the door.

I repeated myself.

"For sho," Keith said with a little country grammar. He laid a big wet one on me.

"I don't need to see all of that. Chante, don't you want to keep Lil Shawn and Shana overnight?"

"Nope."

"Come on, Chante. You and Keith can play house."

"We play house just fine."

"I have not had a full night's sleep in four weeks."

"You should've thought about that before you had sex. That's all a part of being a mommy."

"I don't need jokes right now. I need a full night's rest."

"When you wean them off of the breast, they can spend the night." I laughed. I knew Kayla planned on breastfeeding for a year.

"I can pump milk into a bottle."

I answered the ringing phone, "Yes, Franklin?"

"Kayla, excuse me for a minute." I stood and walked over to the door. "I might have some drama, drama, drama." I said drama like Bernie Mac said 'trouble' in *Players Club.*

"What drama do you have? Don't tell me you and Keith are about to role play with me and my babies here?"

"I'll leave cowboys and Indians to you and your sperm donor. That was Franklin. Jason is on his way upstairs." The doorbell rang.

"Well, I don't have a cowboy hat for nothing, nor do I own the cow print pants with the ass out to wear outside." We both laughed.

"Right about now the outfit is collecting dust," Kayla said as I closed the den's door behind me.

"What's so funny?" Keith asked as he walked toward the front door.

"It's a private joke, do you need something?" I was trying to get Keith to go back into the bedroom before I opened the door.

"I was going to answer the door since you were chit chatting with Kayla."

"That's okay, Baby. Can you go run us some bath water?"

"Is Kayla about to leave?" Keith was growing tired of Kayla, as was I. Ever since the Simone and Shawn incident, Kayla sought my companionship. Almost every day for the last four weeks, Kayla and her babies visited my house.

"In a little while, I hope."

"Yeah, I can do that. Don't forget you owe me a massage. And that means my feet, too." He laughed. Keith knew I hated touching other people's feet.

The doorbell rang again.

"I know. I know." I waited for him to go back into the bedroom before I opened the door.

I opened the door. "Can I help you?"

"Yeah. I thought maybe we could get this right this time. I miss you and I want us." He kissed my forehead and smiled. He placed his hand on my stomach. *Why couldn't he have said this months ago?*

I quickly pushed his hand away. What or whom in the hell gave Jason the impression that I missed him or wanted us. We hadn't spoken directly since the incident in the elevator. That was six months ago. I hadn't craved him since then. His words still hurt. Did he actually forget about the words he uttered to me in my office? I hadn't.

"What gives you the impression that I still want us?" I whispered trying to close the door in his face.

Jason used his weight to brush past me and enter the condo. He placed his hand on my stomach for the second time. I quickly slapped his hand away again.

"Because I love you and you love me. You gone always love me, girl. And I am going to always love you." His lips touched mine before sitting down on the couch.

I hoped and prayed Kayla did not come out of the den. Too late. I saw her eyes peeking through the cracked door.

"Chante...Chante!" Kayla walked into the living room.

I stood in the entrance to the other hallway and was relieved at the sight of my closed bedroom door.

"What's going on here?" Kayla asked. "Are you fucking Jason?"

No Kayla, but six or seven months ago I was.

Jason sat there, anticipating my answer as well.

"Kayla, what the hell are you talking about?"

"Chante, what was all that?" Kayla asked.

If your nosy ass had stayed in the den behind closed doors, I would not be forced to lie to you.

Once again Jason was waiting anxiously for my answer.

"What was all of what?" Jason kissed my forehead. "You don't kiss people on the cheek or forehead?"

That was a good response.

Kayla opened her mouth to speak, but quickly closed it at the sight of Keith exiting the bedroom and coming toward me.

"Kayla left?" He kissed the back of my neck. "Did you get rid of whoever was at the door?"

He never looked up into the living room. That was a good thing.

Damn. He looked up.

"Hey what's up, Jason?" Keith walked into the living room and shook Jason's hand.

Jason and Keith were acquainted due to the industry. However, this was Keith's first time being introduced to Jason as my man.

"What's good?" Jason asked with a phony smile. Fire in his eyes.

I was busted.

Or was I?

Keith didn't have clue. Kayla was working on the exclusive story in her head. I could tell by her eyes. I would worry about her later. It made no difference to me what Jason thought or felt. Jason abandoned his child and me. That's how I felt. I was through with him. We had said our goodbyes that day in my office.

What would make him honestly think I still wanted him? He probably thought I was still pregnant. That would explain why he kept putting his hand on my stomach.

Kayla remained silent. If looks could kill, I would have been dead.

Jason stood to face me. "I only came here to tell you to make Simone the lead. That probably means adding another character. I know you will have to finagle some things, but you can do it. I have put you in more compromising positions, so this should easy for you." He grinned when he said *put you in more compromising positions*.

Was he talking English? Or was he smacking me in the face for no longer craving him.

"The lead in what? I'm not working on anything new."

Jason looked at me as if to say, *you know exactly what I am talking about*.

I shook my head. "Wait a minute. Production began a few weeks ago."

Jason didn't know whom he was messing with.

"Chante, I'll be waiting for you since you're talking business. Kayla, give them some room." Keith left us alone.

Kayla went back in the den with Shana on her shoulder. She left the door wide open and sat on the couch.

"You think I give a fuck about production beginning?" Jason asked. "Production stops when I say it stops. It goes on pause when I say pause. I'm a man that gets what he wants when he wants it. You know that. I give my lady what she wants when she wants it as well. I think your closet proves that along with the valet every time he parks that

Bentley." He sat down and extended his arms up on the couch.

I sat down in front of him on the love seat. "Jason, what is this really about? You and I both know you didn't come here on some make Simone a star bullshit."

"You know what this is about," Jason said sternly.

"You're right. I do," I lowered my voice because I knew Kayla, the nosy best friend, was listening. "You're jealous. How could Chante not want me? I know you are beating yourself up inside trying to figure that one out.

"You knew I wanted a life with you. I told you I would give away all that I had to be a family with you. And you told me that I appeared to be happier with ole dude, to go ahead marry him and let him raise my baby.

"Did you actually think you were going to enter my life six months later and pick up where you left off? You haven't even shown the least bit concerned as to why I am no longer pregnant?"

"Chante, you killed my baby?"

I ignored him and his disappointing look. I smacked his hand away before it touched my abdomen.

"Now, because you're hurt, because it has quickly seeped in that I don't want you, you think that you can make me create a part for Simone. I am not going to hire someone that you fucked in a club or gave you head in your office or someone you bought a car for because you said so." I escorted him to the door.

"You gave me head and I bought you a car."

No, that bastard did not go there.

"Jason, take a good look at who you are talking to. Now take a good look at my ass because on Monday morning you'll be begging to lick it. Now get the hell out of my house."

♫

"So that was your drama?" Kayla walked into the hallway after hearing the front door close.

"That was my drama." I hadn't decided if I was going to tell Kayla the truth or not.

Kayla followed me into the bedroom and sat next to Keith on the loveseat. "Damn."

Keith laughed. His dimples were saying *Chante, come lick me*, as he chilled out in his pajama pants.

"What's good, Kayla?"

"I'm straight." She smiled, eyes never diverting from what she was staring at.

Keith placed one of the throw pillows over his lap. "Kayla, you are such a cock blocker."

"It must run in the family," I joked.

Kayla rolled her eyes.

"Here, take your godson. Teach him whatever sport you're watching." Kayla handed Little Shawn to Keith. She laid Shana down on my bed since she was asleep and practically dragged me out of the room by my arm.

As soon as we entered the den, the smile fell off her face. She began with her twenty-one questions.

"So you're fucking Jason?"

"Kayla, sometimes you put your nose where it doesn't belong." I decided I wasn't ready to be truthful with her.

"So, what are you saying? Kayla, mind your business?"

I didn't respond. I put a DVD into the DVD player and turned the television on.

"Are you telling me to mind my business?" Kayla began to roll her neck, like her name was Rasheedah and I was Tameka and we were getting ready to throw down.

"Kayla, you know what I said and you know what I meant. I choose not to hear your mouth about what I do, so as a result I keep you on a need to know basis. All you need to know is that I am very happy with Keith."

"Well, evidently you aren't happy enough if you're fucking Jason."

No, she didn't just say that. Kayla was two seconds from getting tossed out of my house. She should have thanked the Lord that Keith prevented her from getting bitch slapped by sticking his head in the door when he did.

"Baby, you mind if I come watch a movie with you two, or is this a girl's only event? Shawn fell asleep on me and the game is over. My team lost." His dimples were saying, *pretty please.*

Kayla sat on one side of the sectional looking like she was ready to rumble.

"Keith, can you go pop us some popcorn?"

My tone said a lot. He closed the door and it was on.

"Let me tell you something, don't you dare walk into my house and think you are going to judge me. What I do is my business and my business only. If I share it with you, then and only then does it become your business. If I do not share it with you, then it ain't for you to put yourself into. Like I told your nosy ass before, all you need to know, since your nosy ass needs to know every goddamn thing, is that I am very happy with Keith."

"I wasn't judging you. I'm pretty sure you know what you do and its consequences." She let *consequences* roll out of her mouth. "From what I see, Keith is a good man, and you two seem to do well together, just don't hurt him. You didn't like how it felt when Jason hurt you. And for you to turn around and fuck him just doesn't make much sense."

It was time for Kayla to leave. There was no way in hell I was going to have an argument with my best friend about who I was screwing. As long as it wasn't Shawn, Kayla needed to keep her mouth shut.

"Kayla, it's none of your business who I screw and why. Now, if I want to fuck Jason until I'm blue in the face and come home and suck Keith's dick, that's none of your business." I ended on that note because Keith came into the room.

"Here's ya popcorn. And I brought both of you a bottled water so you don't tell me to get up again." Keith sat in the middle of us. He felt the tension and leaned closer into me.

"Is everything all right?" he asked.

"It is now." I kissed his forehead. "Ain't that right, Kayla?"

"What?"

"Is everything all right?"

"Yeah. Why wouldn't it be?" She had an attitude. But in five minutes, it would be gone and she would be back to herself.

"What movie is this?" Keith asked. He laid his head back on my breast.

Within minutes of watching Tyler Perry's *Why Did I Get Married*, Kayla began making comments about the characters' cheating. I ignored her for as long as I could. After awhile I couldn't take it anymore. Keith sensed it.

"How did you get this on DVD?" Keith asked sensing I was about to curse Kayla out. "I know miss movie maverick, producer extraordinaire ain't buying no bootlegs. This hasn't even come out in the movies yet."

I closed my mouth and turned away from Kayla to look at Keith. Lord knows I love this man. I smiled. I was tempted to rub our love for each other in her face, make her envy what we shared.

"I know someone who knows someone at Lions Gate who got me this complimentary DVD. You jealous?"

"I'll remember that when you want a CD before it comes out. Better yet, guess who won't be going to St. Barts with me for Memorial Day weekend?" He laughed and moved as I swung the pillow at him.

Kayla's comments began again.

"Kayla, you know you don't have to put up with a man that cheats on you," Keith said. "You look good. You can easily go out and find a man. I'm sorry I'm taken. If I wasn't and if I didn't know Chante at all, I would ask for your number." Keith was growing impatient with Kayla.

"What if I told you I wasn't the one in the relationship with the cheater?" She let each word roll off her tongue as if she wanted Keith to really think about it.

"Kayla, get your shit and let's go!" I stood up. I tried my best not to drag her off of the sectional by her hair.

The door flew open and two steaming bitches walked out. Kayla followed me to the front door, which was literally only six steps from the den. As I walked, I debated whether or not I was going to hit her first or talk.

"Look, bitch." Out of my years of knowing Kayla, I had never called her a bitch, not even in play. That was a name we saved for other women. "Why are you so concerned with whom I give my ass to?"

"Who in the hell are you calling a bitch?" Kayla was shouting while her neck rolled.

"You better stop yelling in my house." I hadn't raised my voice, but the bitch knew I wasn't playing. I was fully aware that Keith was within earshot.

"I don't give a damn who your whore ass sleeps with. But I do care if my best friend gets a disease from screwing every dick that comes her way."

"Oh, so now I'm a whore?"

"If the shoe fits, then *whore*, wear it!"

I'd be damned if Kayla was going to tell me off in my own damn house.

"Well, I guess you'll think twice the next time you put Shawn's dick in your mouth, Miss Herpes face, or should I call you Miss Crab mouth?"

BAM! Kayla's bottom lip hit the hardwood floor.

"So I guess you would be concerned about someone catching a disease. Won't you go ask the whore who you slept with where he got his STD's from?"

The fat lady had sung! The case was closed. The door slammed in Kayla's face.

Miss Perfect thought she was bad now since she had been to jail. She pushed the door back open.

"First of all, I am not going anywhere without my babies. I would hate for them to pick up your whoring ways." She stormed past me and walked toward my bedroom.

"Don't worry about them picking it up from me. They'll learn more from their father." I followed her.

"Well, at least I know who my babies' father is, you nasty ass bitch." Kayla's hands were on her hips while her neck rolled again.

BAM! My bottom lip hit the floor. It bounced up and hit the floor again. That was my secret. While I was talking to Jason that child was analyzing everything. She put it all together. Damn her!

"The next time you have an abortion, don't call me because guilt is kicking your ass on the side of the road. Lying to me talking about the baby is gone. Yeah, the little bastard was gone because you sucked him out.

"You got a good man in there that loves the shit out of your nasty ass. He was happy as hell because you were pregnant. All the while you are going along with it knowing good and well, you are not going to have the baby because you don't know if it's his or Jason's."

"Kayla, out of respect for your children I will not knock your teeth out of your mouth. But if you ever utter those words to me or someone else again, you are going to be buying yourself some dentures. Now get the fuck out my house." I extended my arm, showing her the door.

"The truth hurts. Doesn't it?"

Twenty Three

"Chante?" Keith walked into the bathroom fully dressed.

I had forgotten all about my Adonis waiting in the den. A sistah was soaking in the bubble bath drawn for two. All of the stress that Kayla had caused had been soaked away. She really pissed me off. My eyes were swollen and red due to guilt. Relaxation was what I needed. The bath and a drink did the trick.

"Did you forget about me?" Keith asked.

"No. I could never forget about you," I lied. "Get in."

"I can't," he replied coldly.

I was horny. In and out I dipped my finger in the kitty cat. I made sure Keith could see. After each dip I stuck my finger in my mouth. "Why can't you?"

"I have to go pick up Keia."

He appeared to be thinking and speaking at the same time, so his speech was very slow. He was lying. His eyes remained glued to my hands.

"Can you stay a little while longer?"

"No!"

I was not taking no for an answer. So I did the one thing I knew would make him stay. Keith talked as I unbuttoned his belt. He shut up long enough to take a deep breath as he felt the warmth of my mouth. In seconds, Keith's blah blah blahs turned into moans.

"Is there something you would like to tell me?" Keith asked.

Damn. Could I wipe the cum off of my mouth before he went in?

"What?"

Here I sat waiting to be entered while Keith wanted to hold an interrogation. The smile that was just plastered across his face was gone. His business face was on, as well as his pants.

"Is there something you want to tell me?" He looked down at me as if I were his child. He even added bass to his voice when he repeated himself.

"What?" I just licked this man's lollypop like I was the little boy in the tootsie roll commercial trying to figure out how many licks it took to get to the center of the tootsie pop, and Keith hadn't appreciated it.

"Aiight, Chante! Bye."

He turned his back to leave the bathroom.

"Keith!" I shouted.

There was no way in hell he was going to leave me horny like this.

"What, Chante?"

"Where are you going?" I grabbed my towel and followed my man out of the bedroom toward the front door.

"I told you. I gotta go get my daughter." He continued to open the door.

"Keith," I whined.

He closed the door.

In the same spot I had argued with Kayla, Keith kissed me. He pinned me to the wall and my towel fell. He filled my love house with all of his love.

"I guess you're satisfied now?" He zipped his zipper and left.

This sister was sprung. HELL, YEAH! I was satisfied! I wanted to sing "Chante's Got a Man at Home." And I did. When I got to the part about being hurt because your man is leaving you home alone, I thought about it. I was alone. I had given Mr. Pretty Boy one of the best blowjobs he had ever received. I know this because that blowjob bought the Bentley Continental GT parked in the garage. That blowjob should be on the market. It should've also made him stay.

Today was a day of many firsts. Keith never fucks me. He makes love to me. No matter how many times I whisper in his ear for him to fuck the shit out of me, he never has. Keith makes love to my mind, body, and soul. To be honest, I don't need all of that. I would settle for a long tongue to get the waves moving and the magic stick to create the hurricane. Now that I think about it, Keith just fucked me.

"OH MY GOD!"

Had Keith heard Kayla and me arguing? Had he heard the entire conversation? Maybe he just heard the STD part and thought that I had one? *Oh, hell no.* He couldn't think that I had crabs since his face visited south of the border daily. He heard the argument!

"Damn it." I tripped down the stairs trying to get over to the piano to pick up the cordless phone.

My baby thought I was a whore. I had to call him and make sure he was all right.

"What's up?" he answered on the first ring.

"Baby."

"What up, Chante?" His voice was dry and straight to the point. He had definitely heard us. I truly hoped he had not heard the part about the baby.

"Why did you do that to me?" I tried to sound cute.

"Do what, Chante?" His voice was forceful and filled with animosity.

"You know what you did."

"Stop playing with me. What do you want?"

"Why did you fuck me like that?" I could not believe I was asking him that.

"Like what? Stop Keia!" I heard the phone drop.

"Hello...Hello...Keith, Baby?"

"Yeah, Chante." He was more annoyed.

"Baby."

"What, Chante?"

"Why did you fuck me?"

"Isn't that what you wanted?"

"Hey, Tae Tae," Keia yelled in the background.

"Tell Keia I said hello." He did.

"Look I'm only going to ask you one more time. Do you have something you want to tell me?"

I couldn't tell Keith what he wanted to hear. I could say that I was sorry. But I could not come out and tell the man that I love that I had cheated on him, got an abortion, and lied about it.

"Keith, what would you like me to say?"

"I don't want you to say anything." Keith hung up on me.

Never in a million years would I have told a soul that I aborted the baby. I never thought that it would get back to Keith about Jason and me. The fucked up part was that it came from the mouth of my best friend. Quickly, I slipped on a pair of pink Baby Phat sweatpants and zipped up the matching jacket. I tied my Air Maxs and grabbed my car keys. My mission was to kick Kayla's ass.

It was because of her big mouth that my man was hurt. If she wasn't so damn nosy, Keith would still be here with me and we would be happy. But, oh no, because her man was a dog, now she was the national spokesperson for every person who had ever been cheated on.

I drove like a bat out of hell. For each tear I cried, Kayla was going to feel it. How dare her. She came into my home and destroyed all that I had going on. What kind of friend would do that to another? I bailed her out of jail while her baby's father left her pregnant butt there. I later found out by the way of a voicemail message left by Simone that Kayla called Shawn first. I couldn't turn the corner that led to Kayla's cul-de-sac fast enough.

The engine to the Bentley was still running while I was banging on Kayla's door. Kayla was the other woman, the woman who wrecked my happy home. I was going to kick her ass!

The front door flew open.

"Why the hell are you banging on my door like you're crazy?"

"I didn't know you lived here. Nor have I ever known you to pay rent," I said to Shawn. "Where is the mother of your children?"

"She doesn't want to see you," Shawn said as he held the front door open.

"Are you leaving? If not then close the door." I walked through the house looking for Kayla.

My best friend sat in the mahogany rocking chair that I bought her as a gift, rocking her first born to sleep. So many different emotions went through me. I watched her place Little Shawn in his crib. She then turned to the other crib to pull the blanket over Shana. As soon as she looked up at me, her innocent eyes stared into eyes of fire.

I grabbed her by the collar, preparing to swing her ass all around the nursery. Out of the twenty something years I had known Kayla, I had never hit her, and was not going to start today. As I let go of her collar, Shawn walked up behind me uttering some nonsense. Kayla had not said a word. She just leaned against the brown wooden stained doorframe and watched me walk down the stairs.

Kayla was not my enemy. She didn't hurt my man. I did. Eventually the truth would have come out. Of course, then we would have been married for about twenty-five years and had a few babies of our own, so it wouldn't have been that big of a deal. I wanted to be laid up in my man's arms. Sistah girl was not going to rest until I had my Adonis back at home.

The silver Bentley dipped out of one lane and dashed into another. I pressed harder on the gas pedal. Damn a ticket! I didn't give a damn if Mr. Policeman pulled me over.

My man was worth the price of any speeding ticket. As soon as I hit Park Avenue, a smile of relief came over my face. I parked in a no parking zone, right in front of Keith's building. My purse was on the front seat. My keys were still in the ignition, as I stood in the lobby and waited for the elevator.

"Ms. Chambers," the doorman called out to me. "You can't park there. You are going to have to move your car."

"Tow it!" I stepped onto the elevator.

"Do you want me to move it?" he asked as the elevator doors closed.

Damn it! How the hell was I going to get into the penthouse without my keys? I was contemplating going back downstairs to get them. But what if Carl, the doorman, took me at my word and towed my car? I doubt he moved it since I never answered him.

I began banging on the door and screaming out Keith's name a million times. He never answered. With puffy red eyes and tears still streaming down my face, I entered the elevator. I did not stop crying when Keith's neighbors joined me. I actually laid my head on the shoulder of some lady. She smiled at me and politely moved away from me. An older lady handed me her handkerchief.

"Honey, did you catch him with another woman?"

Was the old lady talking to me? I just stared at her as I blew my nose in her Chanel handkerchief.

"You know I came home one day early from the Hamptons, and I caught my first husband, Bradley with a whore. I didn't cry. You know what I did?" Grandma rubbed my shoulder.

My expression showed I didn't give a damn.

"I divorced his ass. When the judge awarded me with more than half of what he owned, that bastard had a heart attack and died. And you know what?"

What?

"Now I own everything." Her wrinkled face smiled.

"Well, Ma'am, I can't take your same approach."

"Sure you can."

"No, Ma'am I actually can't. I'm the whore," On that note I handed Grandma her handkerchief and prepared to exit the elevator.

Grandma's eyeballs nearly popped out their sockets. She closed her mouth, shook her head, and motioned for me to keep the handkerchief. I stuck the snot filled handkerchief in my pocket. By the grace of God, my car was still outside. It did have a ticket under the windshield wiper, but at least it hadn't been towed. By the time I came back again it probably would have another ticket or even worse, so I decided to park it some place legal. I retrieved the keys from the ignition and went back up to the penthouse.

Keith's penthouse was large. I searched each and every room looking for my baby. I did not find him. I lay in the middle of his bed and decided to wait for him. I waited and I waited and I waited. Four hours later, there was no Keith, just me and all my tears. I wrote him a letter telling him I loved him, I was sorry and asked him to call me. Then I left.

Twenty Four

Sunday was over and there were no calls from Keith. Monday came and went. No call from Keith. Tuesday and Wednesday were the same as Monday. By Thursday, I was ready to die. I cried all day Friday. My eyes were swollen, red and puffy. I could not take much more of this. I became a stalker. I called Keith every day, every hour like clockwork. He never answered or returned any of my calls. I wondered how he was doing. Was he doing as bad as me? I couldn't leave the house. I was devastated. Hurt. Guilty. I was emotionally fucked up. On Saturday I sat in the same spot that I collapsed in on Sunday, in the living room on the couch, right next to the telephone.

The whole week had passed me by. All I could think about were the events that led up to it. Why had I allowed Jason to convince me that we could actually start over, get things right this time? Why didn't I just sleep with him that one night, and kick him out in the morning, never to give my pussy to him ever again?

Why did I want to have something with Jason? What was the need to rekindle the flame? Why wasn't my relationship with Keith enough? Technically it was. Keith satisfied me in every way that a man is supposed to satisfy a woman, plus some. With Keith, I was like Whitney Houston singing "All the Man I Need." I left Jason alone. I lived my happy little life with Keith. He was the only man I craved. He loved me, and more importantly I was in love with him. And then here came Jason, wanting us.

Now because of Jason, because of Kayla and of course because of me, my little world has been ripped apart. I could only imagine how Keith felt. To think I let this man believe for months that I was having his baby. I let him believe that I miscarried, knowing all along I aborted the baby. Reliving the abortion had me weeping like a broke prostitute who just got her ass beat by her pimp for coming up short.

How was I going to get my man back? I wanted to throw the ringing phone at the wall. It was making me sick. The same two people kept calling.

"What?" I snapped. I knew from the Caller ID it wasn't who I wanted it to be.

It was Jason calling for the umpteenth time.

"I can't believe you killed my baby. That was you and me. I love you. Why you don't want us? You was just crying telling me you would give up everything if I would do you right. Baby, I'm ready," he pleaded.

I remained silent.

"Don't you know it's going to always be Jason and Chante? I don't care who you fucking. I don't give a damn how big of a ring that man gives you. I could buy you something bigger. I love you. You will always be mine. My name is all over your body!" He had been calling me all week, speaking the same old bullshit.

I hung up the phone. After placing the cordless in the cradle, I decided to just unplug it. Lately, the only time I moved off of the couch was to use the bathroom. However, I was about to get my lazy tail up and unplug all the phones. The only person I wanted to talk to didn't want to speak to me.

♫

A new week had began, beautiful ole me no longer laid on the couch. I had been lying on the floor for the past two or three days. I tried hard to get it together. I had it bad. As bad as Usher had it in "You Got It Bad." In fact I had it worse. I just knew the white carpet was going to be brown from me lying here for so long. But two days later when Keith picked me up from my pool of tears, the carpet was still white, just damp from my tears.

Keith hadn't said a word. Neither had I. I didn't know what to say, so I decided not to say anything at all. He carried me into the bathroom to wash my tear-stained face. *God damn!* I caught a glimpse of myself in the mirror. I looked awful. My eyes were bloodshot red and puffy. Let's not even touch on the hair. He unzipped my pink jacket and pulled my matching sweatpants off with a strong yank at the ankles. I guess I smelled because he was running my bath water.

Keith bathed me in silence. Any other time I would be horny, yet the palace wasn't throbbing. It was afraid to throb. I was scared of what Keith might do. I could only imagine what he had been going through these last few days. He was missing in action on my radar, now all of a sudden he was here. As he washed my thigh, my spot tingled just a little. I smiled. He did not.

"Get up!" He finally spoke.

My expression said *excuse me*. The tears were gone, yet sistah girl hadn't completely lost it. Keith looked down into my big brown eyes as if to say I dare you to say anything. I got up. I wasn't stupid.

Keith wanted me. I could tell by the way he looked at my naked body. His smirk told me he wanted to feel my insides. I wanted him to just hold me, tell me he had forgiven me, and that everything would be all right. If sex was what he wanted and needed, I would oblige. He began to rub spots he knew turned me on. His hand cupped my voluptuous backside and gave it a squeeze.

As I stood in the tub, eyes closed, teeth biting into my bottom lip, Keith's hands explored me. Softly his lips pressed against mine. I pushed my tongue between his lips. I put my all into the kiss. I pulled off his shirt. He dropped the towel he was holding. I undid his belt and his pants fell quickly. Keith returned my kisses with the same intensity.

He laid me down in the middle of the bed. He kissed my lips. Slowly he nibbled at my ear. He left kisses all over my neck and shoulders. His tongue occupied my right nipple while his fingers played with the left one. He kissed one. He kissed them both. His tongue journeyed from my breast to my navel. It made circles around my clitoris. My thighs shook as I clenched the sheets.

"I love you," I said.

Keith did not say a word. He continued on his journey to my toes. He didn't look into my eyes, as he normally did, when I took him into my mouth. In fact he kept his eyes closed the entire time. I stopped concentrating on his love muscle and began to kiss him. I loved him. I loved everything about him. I sucked him again. I needed this. I needed to feel Keith inside of me.

With each stroke I put all my love into it. I rode Keith like he was the last man I would ever ride. I didn't even budge when his juices were released; I continued to roll my hips. I was never letting go of Keith again.

My body fell limp against his. My heart beat on top of his. He held me. I cried. He just held me tighter.

"I love you," I said once again.

Keith said nothing. His embrace said it all.

"Where are you going?" I asked. I was in the bathroom for all of three minutes. When I came back into the bedroom, Keith was fully dressed.

What kind of game was he playing? We had just laid side by side in silence for over an hour. I enjoyed every minute of it. I thought he had, too.

"Kayla called me. She said she had been trying to reach you all week. And she couldn't get through. She knew if she came here, you wouldn't see her. So she asked me to come check on you. I checked on you. You seem all right to me." Keith was serious.

"Baby, we just made love," I pleaded. I looked into his eyes to see if he truly felt nothing for me. I followed him to the front door and searched his face for some type of emotion. I found none.

"Keith, damn it, would you stop!" He closed the front door and turned to look at me. "Keith, I love you. I miss you.

I want you. I'm sorry I hurt you. Would you please forgive me?"

I cried. Keith laughed.

"I thought you loved me?" I held him.

"I thought you loved me, too. But we see how much that was," He pushed me off of him. "You know I can't resist that." He pointed down to the palace.

I grabbed my man. I was not letting him go. I nestled my face into his chest and cried. Keith held me for what seemed like eternity, but was actually two minutes. Then he left.

Twenty Five

"Hi Chante," Dr. Blue greeted me as I walked into her office. She looked me over. Her facial expression said, *Damn!*

I wasn't the Prada princess I normally am. A bitch had problems. My wardrobe proved it. I had washed only twice in the past two weeks. The first bath was the bath that Keith had given me. I couldn't bring my stinking ass out the house without washing today. I showered, threw on some jeans, a white t-shirt and slipped my feet into my Gucci sneakers. I used an old remedy of hair grease, water and a brush to tame my mane into a ponytail.

Dr. Blue shocked me by agreeing to see me, given the fact that I went off on her during our last visit. Then again maybe she was only interested in how my song ended, so she rearranged her schedule to fit me in. Ole nosy heifer. I had been an emotional wreck since everything happened. I wanted to blame everyone except myself for my troubles. Anyone who looked at me funny or said anything that I interpreted as sarcasm was going to catch it. It was time for me to reevaluate myself. I was the one who reached out to her, so I put those thoughts into my pocket for another day. I needed someone to talk to.

"Thanks for rearranging your schedule to fit me in," I said as I made myself comfortable on the couch. I looked down at my propped up feet, and I realized I had on mix matched socks. Oh well.

"It wasn't a problem." She sipped her coffee and smiled. "So, Chante, what brings you here today?"

"Dr. Blue, I have problems! I truly fucked up. My cheating and lying has caused me to lose the love of my life. Before I begin my saga, let me first apologize again for blowing up at our last session."

"That's okay, Chante. I could see that you were going through a lot. I only wished I could've done more to help you." She handed me a tissue to wipe the tears that were beginning to fall down my face.

"You were right."

She raised her eyebrows at me. *Yes, Chante Marie Chambers can admit when she is wrong and someone else is right.*

"What do you mean?" She smirked.

I returned the smirk. "You suggested that we come up with ways to tell Keith the truth. I didn't listen. I thought I was protecting him by hiding the truth. But truth be told, I was protecting myself."

She wrote something down on her notepad.

"Dr. Blue, Keith knows that I killed the baby and he hates me. To be honest I don't know if he's more upset because I cheated or because I got an abortion." The tears began to pour. "Keith made love to me last week. I gave that man all I had between my thighs. I gave him all of me. Gave him my heart. I told him I was sorry.

"And just like that he tells me the only reason he had sex with me was he couldn't resist my love palace. Do you know how that made me feel? I felt like garbage thrown in the street. I still do. I feel like a fool or something. For the first time in my life, I really feel like a hoe, a dumb hoe at that. I love Keith to death. I want Keith. I am truly sorry I hurt him. I apologized to him. Why is that not enough?"

"Chante, did you tell Keith why you aborted the baby? Did you tell him that you were unsure of who the father was?"

"Hell, no, I didn't tell him that. I can't tell him that every chance I got I bounced on Jason's dick like it was a pogo stick. I can't tell him that after I left him in Miami, I came home and screwed Jason the same day. I can't tell him that I had unresolved feelings with my ex and as result I rekindled the relationship.

"How do you tell the man you love that the baby you're carrying isn't his? I can't tell him that his love was not enough to keep me faithful and honest. I misled this man into believing he was going to be a father. I allowed him to bond with this child. I allowed him to take a picture of my pregnant stomach each month. How do I say, baby, as soon as you left for LA, I went to the abortion clinic?

"Dr. Blue, Keith left LA as soon as he found out the baby was gone. My man left his business and rushed to be by my side. He blamed himself for leaving me. As if his absence had something to do with my so-called miscarriage. In all honesty, whether Keith left for LA, or nowhere at all, I was still going to get an abortion.

"I haven't been to work in three weeks. Technically, I haven't spoken to Keith in three weeks, and I haven't spoken to my best friend either. I'm mad at her. Yet, I'm the one who did wrong. I put her on blast, and came this close..." I showed her how close I came with my fingers, "to kicking her ass, for putting herself in Keith's shoes."

We sat in silence for the duration of my hour-long session. Dr. Blue asked a few questions to get me to talk. I wasn't interested. I wasn't there for help. I was there to talk. I needed to get some things that I had been holding in off my chest. She was the perfect person to listen. At the end of the hour, I slipped my feet back into my sneakers, grabbed my Gucci bag and headed toward the door.

"Chante, if you ever need to talk, I'm here for you." She smiled.

I turned to look at her. "Dr. Blue, I just want things to be the way they were before the madness began."

As I walked to the parking garage, the air felt good blowing against my face. The sun shined so bright and everyone around me looked happy. One carefree woman carrying a briefcase smiled at me. I smiled back. It felt good to smile again.

I didn't want to go home. I sat behind the wheel of my car and rested my head on the steering wheel and allowed the last set of tears to fall. I found the quickest exit out of the city and headed to Jersey. I seemed to have no control over what was going on in my life. It was time to regain control. What better place to start than with a massage, manicure, pedicure, facial, and hairdo.

"What the hell happen to you?" Mecca asked as soon as I walked into *With a Little Jazz*.

"Just shut up and do my hair." I rolled my eyes at Mecca and sat in her chair.

"Are you sure you want to start with your hair?" She let

my hair out. In the mirror, I saw her frown as she caught a glimpse of my new growth. "Your eyes are all puffy. You need the works, baby."

Mecca was lucky I loved her. If I didn't, she would have been the first one to catch my wrath. "Let the pampering begin."

I felt like a million bucks after my trip to the spa. My skin was glowing. My fingers combed right through my mane, no more getting stuck in the new growth. No one could look at my eyes and tell that I had been crying for weeks.

A Kool-Aid smile spread across my face at the sight of the Bloomingdale's sign. The shopping sistah was back. For every outfit I purchased, I bought matching shoes and accessories. Was I finished shopping? In the words of Whitney Houston, hell to the no! I was however finished with Bloomies. Now it was time to visit Burberry for a bathing suit or two. A sistah left one store and walked right into another. I left Macy's and headed to Neiman. After BCBG, I made my way to Nicole Miller. I bought a trinket or two from Tiffany's. When I arrived at Gucci with my Nordstrom shopping bags, my luggage was waiting for me.

I had one more item to purchase before my shopping spree would be complete. However, the store I was looking for was not in this mall. I packed all my shopping bags into the car and headed to my next destination.

"Welcome to Liberty Travel, can I help you with something?" A woman smiled from behind her desk.

I smiled. "I need a trip to somebody's island and I must

leave tonight." I handed over my corporate American Express card with a smile. I never left home without it.

Twenty Six

Every time I blinked I was one step closer to dreamland. Once or twice I had actually nodded off. For the last hour and a half, I had been battling sleep instead of watching this footage. Although unedited and incomplete, moviegoers would either nod off or get up and leave the theater, based upon my reaction. It sucked. It was not the same script I approved months ago.

"Where the heck is my red pen?" I said out loud as I searched my desk for it. It was time for a sistah to get into creative mode.

After I found my red pen, I sat down on my new chocolate couch, courtesy of my shopping spree, and began to do what I did best. It was time to get back into the swing of things. For the last month, all I thought about was Keith. I had done any and everything in my power to get my mind off of my Adonis. Nothing worked. Sleep served as temporary relief. Yet, once asleep I only dreamed of him. I had a movie to produce, so I knew work would help get my mind off of Keith, at least for eight to ten hours a day.

I kept pressing pause and taking notes, referring to the script and making changes. We didn't have much time. The way things were going it looked like we should go back to the drawing board. After thirty minutes or so, I was once again fighting the sandman. I looked down at the pile of pages that I had changed and then at the number of pages I had still had to go through. Forget it! I let the sandman beat me. A sistah kicked off her Jimmy Choo sandals, unbuttoned the True Religion jeans, and made herself more comfortable on her new couch.

♫

"Hey Beautiful," Keith smiled at me as he held a bouquet of tulips.

My face lit up at the sight of my man holding my favorite flowers.

"What's up, baby?" I greeted him with a kiss.

In a dimly lit booth my hands held up my smiling face. I couldn't stop smiling. I loved this man who was profusely apologizing for being late. The more he apologized the harder I smiled.

"Why are you smiling so hard?" he asked, showing his dimples.

"Because I love you."

"I love you, too."

We kissed.

I played with the curls that framed my face and smiled.

"Did you order?" Keith asked looking at the menu.

"What I want isn't on the menu."

"What do you have a taste for?"

"You." I grinned.

"Is that so?"

"Yes, sir."

"Well, I planned on eating you for dessert. I have no

problem having dessert before dinner." Keith stood, pulled my chair out, and reached for my hand.

Something happened when I reached out for his hand. My fingertips caressed the palm of his hand. They stroked his fingers all the way to the tips. When we began to interlock our fingers, the restaurant became crowded. People walked in between us and broke our connection. Jason appeared. He slapped me on my ass and told me it would always be his. I twirled around in circles looking for Keith. In a booth I saw Todd doing what he did best. Right next to him was a woman that looked like me. Her dress was hiked up. Her legs were spread wide open. Her hands rubbed her spot, while her date, Todd, sat next to her pouting.

I shook my head to clear my mind of that image. The restaurant was so crowded; I could not find him. I pushed my way through people looking for Keith. Where had my man gone? I had not gotten a chance to tell him how much I loved him. He was gone and so were the flowers he gave me. The bouquet had disappeared out of my hand just like that. My engagement ring also vanished. What the hell was going on?

"Keith. Keith," I shouted.

I woke up. I looked around at my surroundings. I was in my office, still lying on the couch. I felt a sigh of relief when I glanced down at my left hand. The rock was still there, where it belonged.

My trip to Aruba was supposed to cure this. It had done everything but that. I fantasized about being in Keith's arms, staring into his light brown eyes, hearing his voice, and laying my head on his muscular chest. I just wanted to be in his presence. I missed him like crazy. Weeks had passed, and not once had he called me. I must admit I had called him once or twice. Actually, I had called him too many times to mention.

One day, his mother's number flashed on the Caller ID. I smiled as my heartbeat raced. My baby had finally come to his senses. He was ready to forgive me.

"Hello," I answered.

"Let me tell you something, you little cunt!" It was Keith's mother, Rita Simmons.

I was not going to go to hell for cursing out an old lady. Click! I hung up on her. Do you know that woman had the nerve to call me back? Yes she did.

"Hello."

"Do not hang up on me, you loose pussy," she snapped.

I will not repeat what I said to Mrs. Simmons, but please trust and believe me when I say I set the old lady straight.

I patiently waited around the next few days expecting a call from Keith. I just knew his mother couldn't wait to tell him how I cursed her out. He never called. Whenever I called him, he hung up on me or he allowed his voicemail to pick up. I began calling the Pretty Boy Palace since I couldn't reach him at home or on his cell. Of course, I had no luck. Each time I called, Mr. Simmons was always unavailable, or Mr. Simmons was in a meeting, or busy, or whatever.

It came down to me just saying forget it. I told myself on a Friday that the pity party would be over on Sunday. And on Monday I was carting my butt back to work.

Rosemary knocked on my door and proceeded to enter, so I quickly ran into the bathroom. The last thing I needed was a rumor surfacing about me crying and looking a hot mess. Thoughts of being without Keith always ended in tears. Rosemary huffed while I took my time getting it together. I finger combed my hair back in place, behind my ears and washed my face.

"Here are the storyboards you requested. Where do you want me to put them?"

She put them in the spot I pointed to.

"Let me ask you a question. Who changed this script?"

"Avery," Rosemary answered.

"Who authorized that?"

I did not recall asking Rosemary to have a seat, yet she was sitting across from me. This meant the explanation was going to be good. More like good gossip.

"Well, with you being out, Cameron was temporarily doing your job. Chante, you and I don't see eye to eye on a lot, but I will take you over that hat box any day."

I'm glad to hear that.

"You know how Jason is." She winked.

I knew how to decode that last sentence. Jason and Cameron were sleeping together As a result, she was moving up in the company. We all knew how Jason promoted from within.

"Jason halted production. He had a meeting with some folks to see how the current script would allow the introduction of a new character, named Simone. He, Cameron, Mike, and Avery came up with some ways to pull it off. He told Cameron that changes needed to be made to the script immediately. He wanted to bring in a new character. So, Cameron gave the script to Avery and told her to be creative. The end result is what you are watching and reading. Bad thing is it's not finished yet."

"Why must there be a new character?" I asked.

"Because Simone wants to be in *The Other Woman*. She wants to *be* the other woman," she said with a wink.

What the F was all the winking about?

"This might be a stupid question, but why are we accommodating Simone?"

"Because you and Jason are beefing," she bluntly said.

"What?"

"You've been missing in action. And Jason has been an asshole. Chante, don't look at me like that. It's the truth. You know how gossip is around here. We all know you and Jason share a *thing*, and lately we know that you two haven't been sharing it. We all know that we should never say or do anything against you because Jason will rip us a new one.

"We all know that you run this, and Jason is the front man, he gets all the credit and pays for everything, but you do it all. We know this. Lately, things just haven't been the way we know them to be. So one can conclude that something ain't right between Chante and Jason."

In this one conversation, she had informed me that Jason's World, both professional and personal, was falling apart. My ex lover was screwing Cameron, trying to create another me. I already knew about Simone, and Rosemary knew I knew. To make matters worst, he followed through on his threat. Damn him!

"I've been questioning a lot. Because I know how you operate. Jason said you were aware of it."

"He did, did he?" I nodded my head as it sank in. Only

Jason could and would do this. I am the head B-I-T-C-H. Nothing goes down unless I okay it. What made me the Queen of the Empire? It had nothing to do with the fact that I fucked the boss or that I have the bomb ass twat. I made this company. If it were not for me, my ability to write a script, or my concept of coming up with blockbuster hits, Jason's behind would still be making music videos. His job was not to mess with me, or anything I came up with as long as I stayed within the budget he allowed.

"Don't be grinning at me?" I said as I entered Jason's office. I mumbled to myself during my entire elevator ride up to his office. A bitch was steaming and here he was grinning like a jackass.

"I can't grin?" He smirked so hard I thought his face would burst. "So what brings you back to work?"

"The question should be who the hell gave you the right to change my script and cast that slut as my leading lady." My finger was in Jason's face.

He backed up, walked around his desk and sat down. He motioned for me to take a seat. I did.

"Unless you haven't noticed, the name of this place is Jason's World."

"Since when did that mean anything? If it weren't for me, where would you be? Making 50 Cent videos, directing hoes on how to get their eagle on for Nelly?"

He laughed. "Tae Tae-"

I immediately cut him off. "Don't Tae Tae me."

"If it wasn't you, it would've been someone else."

"Fuck you, Jason!"

Jason watched as I grind my teeth, clenched my fist, and

did anything to stop the steaming bitch from boiling over. He smiled the entire time. Son of a bitch! Then he hit me with the bullshit.

"I've been thinking. The changes that bitch Cameron made suck. She damn sure ain't you. Your script was much better. Although my decision is going to put me over budget, extend production, and we have to start over, I am going to go with the original script that you created. So tell Brandy she's out. I want you to cast Simone in the starring role." He propped his feet up on his desk and leaned back in his chair.

"Jason, that child can't act no more that you can."

"Like I said, it's my movie. I'm paying for it and I want Simone as the lead."

"Don't try to pull rank on me, Jason. The only reason you're so damn adamant about giving her the part is to get back at me. Because I don't want to be in a relationship with you, you would rather mess up a movie that you are going to spend millions to make just to get back at me. Come on, Jason, how much sense does that make?

"There are other ways to hurt me. How about calling me up to your office again while Simone is on her knees sucking your dick? Maybe this time I can watch her swallow? Or how about this, I'll tell you I'm pregnant again, and you can tell me how *I* cheated on you with a man that makes me happy. So I should just marry him and pass your kid off as his. Even better how about you bring your tired ass over to my house unannounced and turn my world upside down again?"

Jason was full of it. I was not going to give Simone a part

in her hair let alone in a movie. My movies were my baby from start to finish. There was no way in hell Simone was going to star in anything I put my name on. At that very moment, I realized Jason was put on this earth to make my life miserable.

"Cast the girl for the part," he said firmly.

I stood. "Is the pussy that good that you want to make this non-acting cunt a movie star? She sucks your dick that well that you'd shell out millions to make a movie that's not going to earn shit at the box office? You do remember that *Glitter* something movie? Was that a hit? Is that what you are trying to duplicate?"

"Make her an offer."

"No! I'm not going to cast her for something just because you fucked her or because you told me to do it."

"Cast the girl and make her an offer." He stood.

"You said it's your shit. You make her a fucking offer." My hand was on the doorknob.

"I already told her she has the part. But I want you to personally make her the offer."

I slammed the door shut. "No you don't! You want to humiliate me. Jason, I will quit before I make her a fucking offer, or cast her non-acting ass to get my coffee. I'm not like you. I give out parts and jobs based upon talent and qualifications. Not because I slept with the person."

"How do you think you got this job?" he asked with a smirk.

I couldn't believe he just said that.

"Jason, don't even go there. You and I sleeping together was not a goddamn job interview. We slept together for old time's sake. Even if you would like to believe that our sexual encounter was a goddamn interview, then why did you hire me and why am I still here?"

"Cause your stuff is good, and I love you."

Jason knew nothing about love. Deep down inside, I still loved this man. I no longer craved him, but I did love him.

"So I am only here because you love me and my pussy is good?"

"You do good work."

"I wish I never met you!"

"Chante, do you think you get away with all the shit you do because you do good work? Because you are just that good. You are the only person that charges vacations, couches, and shopping sprees on my American Express. The one I have to pay for. I am still trying to figure out what the hell is the research that you do damn near every week for five hundred dollars a pop. Man I'm spending thousands on Prada, Dolce and Gabbana, Chanel and other designer shit because I love you."

Oh really. So, my theory about him fucking some girl up in Prada who gave discounts was wrong.

"You love me, yet you want to humiliate me by making me give a job to a heifer I caught giving you a blowjob? You love me yet you tell me you hired me because my pussy is good?" I began to cry.

"Where is the love in that? Jason, all I have done for the past eight years was love you. You cheated and I continued to love you. Never once have you apologized."

"I bought you gifts."

It was now or never. I was finally able to tell Jason

exactly how I felt and he was going to listen.

"Gifts don't keep your dick in your pants! Nor do gifts disrespect you time and time again!"

"But I loved you and my heart is with you. My heart is still with you." He emphasized the word *still.* "I thought this time we could get it right. Get married. But once I saw you with ole pretty boy I knew that wasn't going to happen."

"When were we going to get it right? In between you screwing Simone and buying her a car? Or did I have to wait for you to finish getting a taste of the new fish?"

Jason raised his eyebrow.

"I know about you and Cameron. She brags about it like she doesn't know who I am. Jason, if you wanted to make a comeback, you would've done so when I told you I was pregnant with our child. Being my husband and a being a father were the farthest things from your mind."

Jason attempted to wrap his arms around my waist in a loving embrace.

"Don't believe that. Chante, when I saw that ring on your finger, I was hurt. It was hard for me to accept the fact that you were really serious about another man. Honestly speaking, in the end I was going to make you my wife. Ain't no other woman ever touched me the way that you have."

For a brief moment, I tried to rewind time to a time and place where everything Jason had just said would have made a difference. As my head rested on Jason's shoulder, his Sean John jacket soaked up my tears. I smiled. Then I opened my eyes because I no longer lived in the past. It was time to let go of my love for Jason and move on.

I gazed into Jason's eyes and smiled. My lips pressed

against his in a peck. Damn a peck. I slipped him some tongue.

"I will admit that I enjoyed every minute of being with you again. But, Jason, you will never be the man I need or want." I smiled at the thought of Keith. "I made a decision, and it isn't you." I shook my head. "I don't want this anymore. It's time to go. Take your role, Simone, your bullshit lies and this damn job and shove it up your ass!"

I was through with Jason's World.

Twenty Seven

"Chante!" A beautiful little girl with a wild ponytail ran into my arms.

We hugged. "Hey, Keia."

Her eyes brightened when she saw me. "I missed you so much."

"I missed you, too." We hugged again.

I stood up to acknowledge her mother, Nicole, who was browsing through a rack of clothes.

"Hello, Nicole. How are you?"

"I'm doing well and you?"

My expression said it all.

"I guess we have something else in common, too." She grinned.

The old me would have cursed her out for assuming anything. Yet the new me accepted things for what they were. We were both guilty of cheating on Keith.

"Who told you?"

"You know Rita called and gave me an ear full." She picked up a pair of Donna Karan linen gauchos and held them up to her waist.

"I didn't know you talked to her like that." I admired the gauchos on her. I swear Nicole and me could've been the best of friends. Her style had Chante written all over it.

"That looks hot with this shirt." I held up an orange halter-top.

"I don't." She took the shirt from me and held both pieces in front of her.

"Keia, ask the salesperson to put this in a dressing room for me." She handed the clothes to Keia and waited for her to leave our presence before she spoke again.

"Rita called me and cussed me out for being a slut and fucking up her son's life. Because I was a whore, he had to run into your loose pussy ass and have his heart broken.

"Chante, I wanted to come through the phone and just smack her in the mouth for the things she was saying about me, but I wanted to get in my car and drive to her house and punch her in the mouth for the things she said about you.

"Chante, you are the first woman Keith has ever introduced Keia to. And I know you are not the first woman he has dated since we broke up. So that means something. You make my child happy. And I know you have her best interests at heart. I know it was your idea for all of us to spend Christmas together.

"You brought the best out of Keith. Personally I think his mother has more influence over him then he would like any of us to believe." She looked up from the rack of clothes and stared into my eyes.

"I could not allow that woman to say the stuff she was saying about a person my child loves. So I told her to shut the fuck up. I asked her did she forget that she cheated on Keith, Sr., and Keith was not his so-called father's son."

My bottom lip hit the floor.

"I guess you didn't know that," she said. "Well he's not.

But in any case, she is no better than the rest of us. So she is in no position to judge any goddamn body."

Nicole smiled at the return of Keia, who she could tell was eavesdropping.

"Chante, can you come to my dance recital on Saturday?" Keia held my hand and smiled the prettiest smile. "I tried to call you to invite you, but my daddy wouldn't give me your new number."

"My new number?"

"He told me you changed your number." She made a face that only a child could make knowing her father was feeding her some bullshit.

I looked up to Nicole for some of her insight on whether I should agree to come or not. She smiled and nodded her head.

"I wouldn't miss it for the world."

"Mommy, do you have a piece of paper and pen? Chante, give me your new number."

"Chante," Nicole called as I walked away.

I turned around. "He still wants you."

She gave Keia a few more items to give to the sales lady. Then she walked toward me. "Keith never looked at me the way he looks at you. His eyes twinkle since you entered his life. Right now they are little dim, but they twinkle all the same. Keith is stubborn, and you know that. He needs a little time. He'll want to see you at the recital."

"Thank you."

I paid for my items and left.

It was good to know that deep down inside of Keith a flame still burned for me. The feeling was mutual. I wasn't going to push myself onto Keith. However I planned on looking HOT! So hot that he wouldn't be able to resist a sistah. That morning, I was Mecca's first client. She styled my hair in big sexy curls, just the way Keith liked it. Gina accented my natural beauty by coloring my face in earth tones. My fingernails and toenails adorned a French design.

Once again instead of getting dressed, I was watching videos in my dressing room. Heather Headley's, "In My Mind" had me glued to the screen. Sean, a stylist at *With a Little Jazz*, called this song the crazy psychotic woman's song. I laughed when he said it, and I laughed again now as I listened to the words of the song. He was right. I guess I was a crazy psychotic woman, for years in my mind I would always be Jason's girl. That crush had ended and a new one began. Keith would always be the love of my life.

"They say if you love someone you've got to let go," I sang with Heather. "And if it comes back it will mean so much more."

Heather was right. I smiled.

In one hand I held my white pants suit while my gold sandal was on my left foot. In the other hand I held my black skirt suit while a silver sandal dressed my right foot. I glanced at the clock and realized that time was not on my side. There was no way I was going to make it to the city in an hour unless I walked out the door now. Given the fact that I was standing there topless in some boy shorts meant I was going to be late.

"Excuse me," I said to Keith as I slid into the row. There was an empty seat between Nicole and Keith, reserved for me.

My heartbeat began to race at the sight of Keith.

"Chante?" He was surprised to see me.

He glanced over at Nicole, who would not look in his direction. Then he looked at his mother, whom I heard call me a bitch. Yet her name-calling meant nothing once Keith looked at me again. Keith remained silent, yet his stare called me beautiful, sexy, and gorgeous. The white pants suit with the silver sandals had been a good choice. I must admit I accessorized very good with my Dior chandelier earrings and a platinum butterfly necklace that dipped down into my exposed cleavage. I was sexy. Not x-rated sexy, but very sexy for a dance recital.

"You're late," Rita barked.

"Hello, Rita. How are you?" I sat. "It was not my intention to be late. The traffic at the tunnel was ridiculous."

Someone sitting in the row in front of us turned around and shushed me. I gave her a look to tell her she was messing with the wrong sistah.

I sat with my right arm touching Keith's arm for two hours. I was in heaven. The only time we didn't touch was during the fifteen-minute intermission.

"Chante, did you see me?" Keia ran up to me in one of her five costumes.

"Yes, I saw you."

"She almost missed you," Rita mumbled.

Nicole and I both rolled our eyes at her.

"I told you I wouldn't miss you for the world." I hugged her and handed her the sunflowers I brought and a small Dior bag.

"Dior for me?" Keia smiled opening the bag and taking out the box.

"Keia, is Chante the only person you see?" Keith asked, handing his daughter a bouquet of pink roses.

"Daddy, you know I always save the best for last." She kissed his cheek and continued to open the Dior box.

"Oh look, Daddy, look Mommy, Chante bought me earrings."

I was happy to put a big smile on Keia's face. Keith never spoke to me, but his eyes said it all. He was happy to see me.

"Keith, Keia and I ran into Chante at Donna Karan, so we were able to invite her to the recital after all." Nicole smiled and then winked at me. "That was a good thing since you couldn't find her new number, right?"

Keith rolled his eyes at Nicole.

"Daddy, why did you say Chante's number changed? She told me her number hasn't changed." Keia stood in front of her father with her hands on her seven-year-old non-existent hips.

"Cuz, I'm mad at her, and I didn't want her here." Keith looked me in my eyes as he spoke.

"Well, Daddy, she's not mad at me or you. I wanted her here. I love her and she loves me. Chante, would you like to go out to dinner with us?"

I wasn't sure if I should've come to the recital, let alone

go to dinner with them after Keith's last comment. My expression showed confusion.

"I think Chante might have other things to do," Keith responded for me.

I flashed a phony smile. "Keia, your daddy is right. I have some work I have to do. You were the best dancer there. I'm glad you like your earrings. You have my phone number, so do not be afraid to use it."

She hugged me.

"Chante, thank you for coming," Nicole said. Then she hugged me and whispered in my ear. "I'm sorry."

"Your coming meant a lot to my daughter," Keith said and instructed the valet attendant to bring my Bentley.

A tear fell from my eye. I lost my man.

Twenty Eight

India Arie's *Testimony volume one*, played in the background, flames from vanilla scented candles flickered and casted a beautiful silhouette of my friends on the white walls of my living room. I looked at my friends and smiled. As usual, Yolanda was stuffing her fat honey brown face with food. She shook her jet black hair out of her pretty face as she washed her pig in a blanket down with some champagne. Sitting next to her on my new chocolate suede loveseat was Tia. Tia was the hot chick, a shade or two darker than me, five foot five with curves in all the right places. If she poured one more glass of Grey Goose, she was going to the liquor store to buy another. Tia flung her reddish brown and blond Farah Fawcett weave and picked up the bottle of vodka.

"Chante, why are you looking at me like that?" She grinned and poured some cranberry juice into the vodka.

"Look here, diamond princess, your ass is going to be going to the liquor store to replenish my stock."

She waved her ice in my face as I walked over to the front door.

I rushed to open the door with a smile on my face. At last my final guest had arrived. I must admit I smiled from ear to ear when Franklin called to tell me my guest was on their way up. We met each other with a smile. We hugged like we hadn't spoken in years. It had only been a few months since we last spoke, yet it seemed like an eternity. I missed my friend and my friend missed me.

"I have so much to tell you," she said taking her jacket off. "And what's this I heard about you leaving Jason's World? I have to show you pictures of the twins. They have gotten so big."

Kayla was talking forty-five mph in a five mph zone.

"Damn, Kayla, slow down. We will have time to catch up on everything. But first I want to talk to you in private."

Kayla had tried numerous times to apologize to me for opening her big mouth. I had not been trying to accept it. She had sent me tulips with a card of apology. I stomped all over that bouquet, flipped the card over, wrote go to hell and had them returned to her.

The diva always had to make an entrance. I thought the diva was going to be a no show to my life goes on party since the party started at seven and it was 7:45. But just like a true diva, my girl was there bearing gifts. She had a bottle of Moet in one hand and a junior's cheesecake box in the other.

"Hi everybody," she said entering the living room. "What's up, Tia, Yolanda? Oh my God, Mecca you cut off all your hair!"

Kayla ran over to Mecca to get a better look at her new haircut.

"Yeah, I did." Mecca smiled and rubbed her hair. "Tae Tae, where is the cork screw?"

Mecca's mocha brown face looked very pretty with the short 'do.

"That's what I'm talking bout," Tia said. "Tae Tae, do you have some orange juice?"

"The cork screw is in the kitchen on the island next to an empty bottle that you whores drunk up. I did not invite you all over here just to get drunk. So sit back down, eat some hors d'oeuvres and wait for dinner. Aiight?" I pulled Kayla into the den.

"Chante, you don't have to apologize," Kayla said as soon as I closed the door.

"Who said I was saying sorry?" My hands were on my hips, and my neck was rolling.

Kayla's smile disappeared. Her face showed confusion.

"I'm just playing." I laughed. "Damn, girl, stop being so uptight. I do need to apologize. I was being an ass."

Kayla gave me that yes you were expression. I hugged my best friend again.

"Tae Tae, those shrimp were so succulent," Kayla said as she savored the last of her jumbo shrimp.

Kayla, Mecca, Tia, Yolanda, and I all looked like a bunch of stuffed rats. I watched Mecca unfasten the button on her jeans. It was very rare that a sistah cooked. I hadn't had a man in months, so there was no reason to throw down in the kitchen. Until now. I came up with a reason to feast, so who else would I share my newfound self and ideas with other than my closest friends.

"Ladies, if we are all finished eating and Yolanda, your fat ass don't need to eat shit else, let's go in the living room so I can tell you why I invited you all here," I said as I stood.

"Forget you, Chante, I'm sorry we can't all be a size six like you." Yolanda rolled her eyes.

"I don't know about you, but I am a size six," Tia said. "Speak for yourself."

"Shut up." Kayla couldn't stop laughing. "Maybe you were a size six when I first met you, but baby, you have to be at the least a size ten borderline twelve."

We all cracked up as we walked into the living room.

"Don't be jealous because you have all that baby fat and you are a ten. Please trust and believe my sexy ass will never be bigger than an eight." Tia flopped down on the sofa.

Kayla rolled her eyes at Tia.

"Tae Tae, this couch is comfortable," Kayla said making herself comfortable.

"Crate and Barrel. Excuse me for one minute. I forgot one thing." I walked out of the room.

"Okay, ladies, please use a coaster." I returned from the kitchen with a tray of mimosas for my girls. "Wings of Forgiveness" came on. It was the perfect song for the discussion we were about to have.

"I invited you all here for one reason in particular." I sipped my drink and sat down on the chocolate suede lounge chair.

"We all need to apologize to our pussies."

"What the fuck?" Tia busted out laughing.

"Especially you, Tia," I said with a straight face. "We all give our pussies to tired ass men who don't deserve them. They fuck anything and then come home and fuck us. We know this and continue to fuck these men without ever once apologizing to our pussies."

All eyes were on me. Kayla and Yolanda both had confusion written on their faces. Yet the stare I got from Mecca told me she understood.

"Tae Tae, are you drunk?" Tia asked, still laughing.

"No! I'm not drunk." I sat my glass down. "But I know your pussy is tired of you letting everyone who can buy diamonds, Dior, Jimmy Choos, and Manolos up in it."

"Why are you worried about my pussy and whom I give it to? Are you into some lesbian shit now that Keith don't want you?" Tia asked.

"Tia, if you call me a dyke again, I'll cut you. Personally, I don't care who you give your pussy to and the funny thing is I don't think you care either. Months ago I asked Kayla that same question. And do you know what? If I cared who I gave my pussy to, I would be sitting here with Keith instead of you funky whores."

"Did you invite me here to call me a hoe?" Tia asked, getting up.

"First of all, I would never refer to any of us as hoes. But we are whores."

"What's the difference?"

"Whores get paid. I don't fuck anybody for free."

"I know that's right." Mecca gave me a hi-five.

"But in any case, no, I did not invite you here to call you a whore."

"Yes, you did. Come on, Yolanda, let's go." Tia started walking toward the closet to get her jacket.

"T, sit down," Yolanda said. "You all getting up like you drove here. You know you rode with me because you wanted me to be your designated driver, and I'm not ready to go yet.

"Chante is right. We do give our bodies to anyone without any concern for who they've been with or what their intentions are with us. I will settle for good sex with a piece of man, just to say I have one.

"Kayla don't look at me like that, because you are doing the same thing. I go into court and I appear confident like I'm all about my business. And when I am in court, all of that may be true. But I don't have guys knocking on my door because they really want to be with me.

"Men call me because they know my deep throat is what's up and a big girl can work magic with the hips. I know for a fact that I don't give my vagina time to breathe. And I need to apologize to my pussy."

Kayla laughed.

"What are you laughing at, Kayla?" Yolanda asked. "Right now you should be sitting with your legs wide open begging your pussy for forgiveness."

Kayla just rolled her eyes. "You don't know what I say to my pussy."

I laughed because Kayla knew she didn't say anything to her private parts. She should be praying to God and thanking him for it still being there, and in good health.

"I know you didn't say thank you and please forgive me to your pussy or your mouth the day after Shawn had you slurping another woman's ass."

What the hell? My bottom lip hit the floor came back up and slapped me in the face. Did Yolanda just accuse my best friend of participating in lesbian activities? Yolanda was clearly over two hundred pounds; however, I was going to try my best to kick her ass.

"Hold up, Yolanda. Don't start lying on people." I stood up.

"Am I lying, Kayla?"

Kayla's silence said it all. I never knew Kayla had sex with women.

I stared her down. She never looked my way.

"Chante, stop looking at me like that." She finally spoke after I stared her down for a good two or three minutes. "It was only once. And Yolanda, do you really want to expose secrets?"

Since we were exposing secrets, I was tempted to tell everyone my secret. The only one who I told my secret to was Mecca.

"A ménage is not that bad." Mecca took the spotlight off of Kayla.

"You're into that?" Tia frowned.

She nodded.

"Ray wanted to have a ménage. So I did it. We did it with this girl once or twice, and with this other girl. I'm not a lesbian or anything like that. Nor am I a bisexual. I did it with two guys the other day. And it was good. I enjoyed it, and I will probably do it again."

"I hope you used protection." I was one to talk.

"Girl, I use condoms and any other contraceptive on the market. A pregnancy ain't happening for me unless I want it."

I knew that comment was directed at me.

"Well since we all agree that our pussies deserve an apology. Let's apologize." Kayla sipped her mimosa.

Yolanda slid down to the edge of the couch, spread her legs and bent her head down. "I'm sorry. I didn't mean to abuse you."

Mecca also had her head between her open legs. "I'm sorry I've had so many users."

Kayla was in a similar position as Yolanda. "I am sorry I have allowed Shawn to come inside you after being in other women and leaving diseases, sperm and crabs."

I laughed at her comment, but I joined them on the edge of the chair and I apologized to my pussy for never having enough.

"Pussy, please forgive me for subjecting you to dicks that were not worthy of you. Lord knows I am sorry for subjecting you to Todd's quick nutting ass. Please forgive me for allowing Jason to enter you numerous times and making you tingle multiple times…."

We all laughed.

Twenty Nine

As the rain poured down over the city, I watched it. I lay on the chaise with my laptop on my lap and I wondered what Keith was doing. I missed him like crazy. You would think after all these months I would be over him. Especially after he said he didn't want to see me. Yet, ten months later I missed him more than I had the day after our breakup. I had given up my mission of getting my man back after the recital. If it were meant to be, God would bring us back together one day. Right now, Keith didn't want to forgive me. Despite the wrong I did to him, I knew I made a dent in his heart and when he was ready to forgive me he would. In the meantime I had to make something out of my life.

I was a thirty-something, unemployed black woman. I was unemployable. That ole punk Jason had me blacklisted. I felt like Sandra Bullock in the movie *Two Weeks Notice*, when she tried to find another job as an attorney and couldn't get hired by anyone. I refused to go back to Jason's World. He called and asked me on several occasions, even sent some sign on bonuses in the form of Gucci, Manolo, and Jimmy Choo.

I said "HELL NAW," just like Sophia from *The Color Purple*, although I kept my sign on bonuses. The movie that I had been working on was a step above a flop at the box office. Jason's new star was turning into a diva. She kept demanding more and more. Jason had his hands full and needed someone to come run things as only I could. Cameron wasn't me. And because she wasn't, Jason fired her.

I hadn't just been sitting on my butt, watching soaps and getting fat. Well, I did watch Judge Hachette and Mathis, and of course we can't forget about Maury. In between watching television, I had written a few screenplays. I wrote up a proposal, presented it to Chase Manhattan Bank, and guess what? They loaned me enough money to start up Princess Productions.

I was an entrepreneur.

"Go, Chante, it's your birthday. Go, Chante, it's your birthday." I had to get up and do my dance. Every time I thought about it, I smiled from ear to ear.

I looked down at the too small white tank top that covered my breasts and the white panties that covered my butt, yet my butt cheeks hung out. I looked out the window and realized someone might be looking at me. I didn't care. I owned my own production company. I shook my booty some more.

The Bank of New York had turned me down. Bank of America had politely said no. I didn't know what to expect from Chase. I decided to show some legs, so I went there in a professional business suit. Whatever it took to get a loan, I was willing to do. I could not take another rejection. I made sure my proposal was tight. I presented it and in less than fifteen minutes, I had been approved.

"Hello," I answered the ringing phone. If this was the

real estate woman calling for the twentieth time to confirm, I was going to tell her to forget it and call up a different agency.

"May I please speak to Chante Chambers?" a woman asked.

"This is she, whom am I speaking to?"

"Hello Chante. This is Johnna Damsio from HBO."

"Hello, Johnna."

"We had some time to talk since our meeting with you earlier this week, and I want you to know we are interested in picking up your pilot, *Cat and Mouse*. I would like to set up an appointment with you to come in and discuss the specifics."

I screamed right in Johnna's ear, unable to hold my composure.

"Sorry about that, Johnna. You have no clue how happy I am about this. Thank you. Thank you." I hung up the phone.

Shit! I forgot to set the appointment. I was too busy singing and dancing.

"Go, Chante, it's your birthday. Go, Chante, it's your birthday. I switched up the tune adding a little bit of 50 Cent to it. "Go, Tae Tae, it's your birthday. We gonna party likes it's your birthday..." I popped my thang right back over to the phone and called Johnna to set up an appointment for the following day.

I was late meeting Carla, the real estate agent, at the future home of Princess Productions. When I should have jumped my ass in the shower, I was too busy on the phone calling everyone I knew, telling them that they would see my name as executive producer and creator for HBO's newest original series. I was so excited. I wanted to share this joy with everyone I loved including Keith.

I dialed his number, but immediately hung up after the second ring.

Carla was waiting out in the rain for me as I drove up. I would have been pissed if I stood out in the rain for a client that was over forty-five minutes late. Yet, Carla was waiting under her Burberry umbrella with a smile. Maybe it was the huge commission she would receive that had her smiling. She gave me a tour of the five-story building, which had a huge sound studio. She really didn't have to. I wanted this building and what mama wanted mama usually got. Now mama just had to get her man back.

Thirty

I was feeling sexy, just as sexy as Beyoncé was feeling in that "Naughty Girl" song. As the song played, I pretended I was her. I kicked my sud-covered brown leg up in the tub the way she did in the champagne glass. I was no longer Chante Chambers. I was the girl in the video, doing her thing. The song lyrics floated out my mouth. My movements were the same as hers. I taunted and teased my love interest the way she did Usher in the video. I rose, grinded my butt all over Keith's private zone. It was on.

His hand gripped my waist, making the grinding more intense. His hardness rubbed against my sensitive spots causing moisture. I forgot all about Beyoncé and began doing movements of my own. I stood up in the tub with my arm extended. Keith stood behind me holding my hand. He kissed each fingertip. Then he moved on to my shoulders. His tongue explored my body. I tingled in places I never knew would cause that type of effect. It was on the edge of the tub that I opened my eyes and realized that it was not Keith's thumb and pointer finger rubbing my clit. It was my own.

If I couldn't have Keith in reality, I would always have him in my dreams. I switched the song to "Dangerously in Love." I repositioned my foot on the tub, closed my eyes and continued to enjoy the sensations that Keith was delivering.

A smile remained on my face as I lay in the tub rejuvenated. Nothing could take me down from my high. Not only did a sistah just rub herself right, everything in my life was going my way. I still didn't have a man. In the beginning of my song, I was singing "Chante's Got a Man." Well, this Chante had a man. I didn't appreciate him and he left me. For a minute I was singing Chante wanted a man. But I decided to just let it go. My new tune was *Mine Again*, by Mariah Carey. If it was meant for us to be together, then the gods would bring us back together when the time was right. In the meantime I was going to enjoy life.

Cat and Mouse premiered on HBO, last week. The numbers were a hit. Jason fired my stars from *The Other Woman*, the movie I had been producing and replaced them with Simone and Todd. That was fine with me. And I was pretty sure it was fine with Brandy and Troy because they could be seen every week on HBO. As far as I was concerned, my life was right where it should be.

Keith sent me tulips and a bottle of champagne to congratulate me on my success. I thought that was a sign of progress since his card read, 'I still love you'. I guess I thought wrong. I called him last night to thank him, and some woman answered his phone and it damn sure wasn't his mother. I heard the feminine voice say hello, and shook my head in disbelief. Was he really moving on with his life? I hadn't been with anyone else since him. I hadn't even accepted a date from anyone and there had been offers.

"Hello," she said again.

"Hi." It took everything in me not to say, 'Bitch put Keith

on the phone.' "Can I speak to Keith?"

She mumbled some crap and passed the phone to my man.

"Hey, Chante."

"Hey, Baby." I figured I would call him that and see how he reacted. "How did you know it was me?"

"I always know when you call me."

I smiled. "Thanks for the flowers and the champagne. Sorry I couldn't call you earlier. I just got back from LA."

"You're welcome. I caught the show last week. It's good."

"Thanks."

"Let me ask you a question?"

"Go ahead shoot." I was enjoying every minute of hearing his voice.

"Is *Cat and Mouse* about us? You know the girl chasing the guy?"

"No, but the sequel will be."

"Oh, I see you've been busy."

"Yeah, I've been busy, trying to keep my mind occupied with some things and off of other things."

"Well, it's good to hear from you. Keep up the good work."

He was rushing me off the phone. I was not getting off the phone until I knew who the woman was who answered the phone.

"I enjoyed talking to you to. Tell Keia I said hello and your new little friend."

"She's not my friend. She's my stylist."

Stylist my ass. "Is that what we call them these days?" We shared a chuckle. "Bye, Keith."

I didn't even want to think about Keith with anyone else. If he was happy, then I was happy for him. Not! I shook those thoughts out of my head literally. My hair smacked me in the face. It was time to wash my butt, get out of the tub, and get ready for tonight.

♫

Reggaefest was off the hook. Kayla had managed to get four VIP tickets to the event. I was glad she did. The sound of Sean Paul was bumping in Uptowns. Sasha was singing something about still being in love. Me, I was in the same spot I was in an hour before, on the dance floor, winding my hips. We lost Mecca as soon as we entered the club. Kayla and Tia were next to me singing and winding their hips as well. Yolanda was in the VIP section, guarding our gold and Gucci, with an apple martini in her hand swinging the glass in the air. We were having too much fun.

"Damn, Baby. You can wind that body," said a man dripping in Dolce and Gabbana cologne. He grabbed me by my waist and proceeded to dance with me.

I knew that voice and smell anywhere.

"You know how good I am at winding this body. And you know I can wind it all night if need be." As the song changed, I danced to the new beat of Elephant Man.

"That's the problem. You wind it too good. So good that everybody has to have a piece," he said.

I was enjoying grinding my body against him until he made that comment.

"Keith, please don't start." I turned around to face him

and wrapped my arms around his neck. He wrapped his arms around my waist. Together we began a slow grind.

"Let's just enjoy the song, and see where the night takes us." His lips touched mine.

Thirty One

The time on the clock read 10:01am. The bed I lay in was very familiar, yet it was not mine. I loved the scent of the man lying next to me. I glanced over at my Adonis and just smiled. I loved this man. The song we danced to at Reggaefest last night, or should I say this morning led us to another song and on to another song. Once the party was over, it led us to his penthouse apartment.

I had been lying next to Keith's sleeping body for the last five hours. The throbbing of the palace woke me along with the ringing telephone. Keith was still a heavy sleeper; he didn't move a muscle. My Adonis looked gorgeous sleeping. I leaned in and kissed his succulent lips. As a reflex he kissed me back and rolled over. I contemplated answering it. Should I? Shouldn't I?

"Hello?" I answered.

"Hello?" The voice of a woman repeated.

"Yes, how can I help you?" Sistah girl was back. Who the hell was this woman calling my man at ten o'clock in the morning and why?

"Can you put Keith on the phone?" The woman had an attitude.

She had no idea who she was dealing with. I was back. Right back where I belonged. Oh hell no! I was not going to put Keith on the phone. "No, I cannot."

I hung up the phone.

The phone rang again.

"Hello," I said with a smile.

"I asked to speak to Keith, somehow we were disconnected. Can you put Keith on the phone?" I could tell she was rolling her neck the way we sistahs do.

"We didn't get disconnected. I hung up on you," I said and hung up again.

Keith continued to sleep while the phone rang again. Once again I hung up on the woman. There was no way in hell I was going to allow my man to talk to another female, especially not while I was in the bed with him. Next, Keith's cell phone started vibrating across his nightstand and playing "More Money More Problems" by the Notorious BIG.

Maybe I should be polite, answer the phone and say Keith's sleeping. It could be business. Fuck that, if it was business the heifer would just have to wait.

I pulled the covers off of me, walked around the bed, picked the cell phone up, and turned it off. Once again I looked down at my Adonis. He looked so gorgeous. I kissed his lips again. He kissed me back.

In the bathroom, I turned on the shower. Keith had to love me to sleep with my funky butt. We were both sweaty after last night's party. We came home, ate some leftovers and literally hit the sheets.

The steam from the shower immediately filled the large bathroom. As I sat on the toilet, I imagined Keith in the shower, washing his body. I had many memories of

252 | D o n n e i l   D.   J a c k s o n

watching him lather himself up through the foggy glass.

"I see some things never change," Keith interrupted my daydreaming. He walked over to me and kissed my lips. I smiled. He then walked over to the other toilet. With the door open, he faced the mocha wall.

I closed my eyes, envisioned my arms around his sexy back as my fingers dug into his skin.

"You alright?" Keith asked taking off his boxers.   I guess I was envisioning us together a little too long. I smiled. "I'm fine."

"You getting in?" He asked before he closed the shower door.

HELL YEAH! I was getting in. I had waited damn near a year for this moment. The last time I was serviced was the day Keith made love to me and left me. It had been a while. I didn't respond. I let my actions speak for me. Keith's oversized t-shirt hit the floor at the same time as my panties.

I stared into Keith's eyes as he held my hands to help me down the two steps into the shower. His lips devoured mine. He left no spot untouched. He kissed my lips. Nibbled on my ear. Placed soft kisses on my neck. My shoulders felt the wrath of his tongue. My breast begged for his kisses, which he suckled like a nursing baby. Then he stopped.

What happened? I opened my eyes. Keith looked at me grinning. He was standing there admiring my naked body as he always did.

"Is there a problem?" I grinned.

"No problem at all. I'm just trying to figure out what I want to do first."

"Let me help you think about it," I pulled him closer into

me. My lips pressed against his. My tongue played tag with his.

"Pass me the soap."

Keith stood in the middle of the shower as I bathed him. My tongue removed the remaining traces of soap. I licked, sucked and kissed every inch of Keith's body. I loved this man and I was willing to show him just how much. My tongue worked its way from the top of his head down to the bottom of his feet. I licked his head the way Jane licked the part in Big Brother All Mighty's hair, in *School Daze*. Afterwards, a sistah dropped down to her knees and did a little deep throat action. I performed it just the way Keith loved it. I stared into his brown eyes, allowed him to pull my hair and fuck my mouth. I even threw in my signature moves.

I stopped Keith from returning the favor. I wanted him now. I needed to feel him inside me now. A sistah backed him up against the wall, wrapped my right leg around his waist, and put him inside of me.

I couldn't wait to get home from work. I could've left work early if I wanted to since I was the boss. Funny thing is when I wasn't the boss I came and left work whenever I pleased. However, I quickly realized that when your name is on everything, you stay until all is done just to make sure it is all done right. By 7:00 p.m., all was completed to my satisfaction for the day. I contemplated whether I wanted to go home and get some clothes or just go straight to Keith's. I decided to stop at Saks and buy me a few outfits for the week. I still had my American Express from Jason's World. So you know when the cashier asked how would I be paying, I kindly placed the American Express card on the counter.

"Excuse me, Ms. Chambers, but this card has been declined," the cashier said.

"Um…" I read the name on her nametag, "Lisa, can you please run the card again."

She did. Then she picked up the telephone and dialed some numbers. I stood there, gritting my teeth and tapping my freshly manicured nails on the counter.

"Ms. Chambers, do you have another form of payment?" Lisa asked with a smile.

"What's wrong with the card I just gave you?"

"The card has been canceled and reported as stolen. I have been advised to confiscate the card." She cut my card in half.

Now isn't this a bitch? Oh well it was only a matter of time. That damn Jason really knows how to fuck a lady. I mean that literally and figuratively speaking. He knows how to hit a woman where it hurts. I just used that card, last week in Prada and there were no problems.

I was not trying to get arrested for stolen credit cards, so I handed her my Saks charge card. "I misplaced the card last week, and I forgot to tell my husband I found the card. He must've canceled it."

When I walked into the penthouse, Keith was sitting in the music room listening to music with a note pad in his lap. A glass of something sat on the coffee table. I dropped my bags on the side of the couch along with my jacket, picked up his glass, and sipped his Hennessy. I straddled him and placed my lips on top of his. He allowed my tongue to play in his mouth. He also allowed me to unbutton his shirt and take mine off.

"Not right now, Chante." He picked me up and sat me down beside him.

I understood perfectly. My man was working. Not a problem. I wouldn't bother him. I laid my head on his shoulder, stretched out beside him on the white sectional, and drunk the rest of his brown juice.

"I didn't hear the door bell," he said writing something down on his yellow notepad.

"I didn't ring it," I replied.

"Did Maria let you in on her way out?"

Why didn't Keith just ask how did I get into his house?

"Keith I used my key and let myself in." He just nodded. "Was I wrong for doing that?" Keith knew I never gave his key back. I was waiting for an opportunity like today to stick my key in his lock and turn it.

"No, you weren't wrong. I just would've preferred if you called to let me know you were coming that's all."

Call? If Keith wanted to play games we could. However I always win at the games I play. Keith could play fool if he wanted to, but he was my man and I was his woman.

"Ok. Whatever." I mumbled.

"What do you think about this song?" he asked.

"It's not a hit, if that's what you are asking." I could not lie to my man.

"I thought it was just me."

We laughed.

The song switched to another song. We sat in silence and listened to the music.

"Chante."

"Huh, Baby?"

"This morning did my phone ring?"

Should I lie and say no? If I did, I'm pretty sure by now the tramp spoke to him, told him I hung up on her. And then Keith would hate me again for being a liar. So I told the truth.

"Yes, this morning, a woman," I said the word *woman* slowly, "called you. I didn't tell you earlier 'cause you know we got caught up in the shower."

He looked over at me and grinned. I guess he was having flashbacks. Lord knows the palace was beginning to throb.

"Keith, is there any baby making music on this CD?" I asked getting up. I picked up the CD cover. "What's this song, *Let's Make Love*?" I asked switching the song to track number 9.

As the melody began, I danced to the music.

"Dance with me." I smiled, pulling Keith's hand.

"Chante, not right now." Keith pulled his hand away.

I bent down and kissed him. "Are you sure?"

He kissed me back, even gave me a little tongue. "Yeah, I'm sure."

I kissed his neck this time and nibbled at his ear. "Are you really sure you're sure?"

I closed my eyes and threw my head back as he kissed my neck. Keith stood, wrapped his arms around my waist, and danced with me.

As the music played, we didn't speak. We just danced. My head rested on Keith's shoulder while he held me tight. The palace kept rubbing against Keith's soldier. Keith repositioned his hands on my butt and pulled me in tighter. I enjoyed the rhythm we created. I closed my eyes as my wetness began to leak. Keith held me tighter and grinded me slowly. The music faded, our dance was over and track number 10 began.

"I take it you liked that song?" Keith asked sitting back down.

"I did." I sat down beside him. "Who is this?"

"It's a new artist, her name is Shannon. The guy singing on the track is Chauncey."

I frowned. "I hope you plan on calling her something else."

"Yo, I said the same thing in our marketing meeting." Keith laughed.

"So how are you going to market her? Is she going to be sexy like Beyoncé, Rhianna or Ashanti? Or is she more of a performer like Ciara? Or is she like an Alicia Keys?"

"You heard a few tracks, you heard the girl blow."

"OK, Alicia Keys can blow, but her image is not sexy."

Keith got up, walked over to his bookcase picked up a picture frame, and handed it to me.

"What do you think?" he asked referring to the picture of him and some young girl with her arm around his waist.

What do I think? I think this chick needs to get her hand off of my man. I see I am going to have let my presence be known over there at the Pretty Boy Empire.

"Why do you have your face all frowned up?" He

laughed. He knew I was jealous. "Chante, it's not even like that." He kissed my forehead.

"Um hum."

"So tell me what do you think?"

"Where is she from? She looks very country to me." You know women always have to player hate on the next woman.

"I know. I hired Alexis Tate to style her. But other than that, come on help me out. You know a star when you see one. You do this every day. Tell me what you think?"

It took me a minute to fix my face back to the beautiful way it should be. Stylist…Alexis Tate, was that the chick that answered his phone the other night when I called him? Quickly I analyzed the voice of the woman who Keith claimed was his stylist against the woman who called here this morning. Guess what…I came up with a match.

There was no need to hate on Shannon. She wasn't my competition. If I didn't know any better, I would think Alexis was.

"She's attractive. I don't see star when I look at her. But I guess with some tweaking she could be. You need to start in the beauty parlor and throw a perm up in her stuff unless you want her to be a part of the dirty back pack crew."

"The dirty what?"

"Keith you asked me I'm telling you. The girl can definitely sing, yet based upon what I heard she is not going to get any airplay. The song let's make love was very sensual. You know come fuck me like. Then again that could've just been Chauncey." I began to rub his crotch. "Market her as sexy. Change that Shannon crap to Eva or

Asia or some sexpot name, and make sure I get my credit for the consulting services I have provided."

"You'll be properly paid," Keith said using his weight to lay me down on the couch. He began to bite my nipples through my bra.

"Baby, you need to get some new song writers and write some better songs..." Keith cut me off by putting his tongue in my mouth.

"Damn, Keith, you almost chocked me," I said, pushing him off of me.

"I'm sorry, Lex, we can talk business later."

"Who the fuck is Lex?" My five-foot-seven frame managed to push Keith's two hundred and something pound body off the couch. "If you forgot, my name is Chante." I grabbed my shirt from the hardwood floor.

I was not going to give Keith the satisfaction of knowing that I was crying. I fought the urge; I picked my jacket up and shopping bags, all the while holding back my tears.

After the front door slammed shut behind me, the tears fell. Keith was no longer my man to claim.

Thirty Two

"Kayla, he had the nerve to call me her name," I shouted into the phone. Kayla wasn't hearing me. She kept saying it was an accident. Of course it was an accident, but it was the principle. Maybe she liked it when Shawn called her some other woman's name, I didn't.

"Tae Tae, calm down. It's not the end of the world."

"Kayla, it's the end of my world with Keith in it."

"Tae Tae, I told you not to go home with that man. When will you learn all men want from you is your pussy? And that's because you give it to them. You should've brought your ass home with me and Yolanda last night."

"Kayla, not now!"

"Alright. Tae Tae. Let's change the subject. Did you have sex with him? This is you, of course you had sex with him. Was it good after all this time?"

I let her diss fly over my head. I didn't feel like arguing. "It was good."

My call waiting alerted me that I had another call. I did not want to speak to the caller, nor did I wish to continue my conversation with Kayla. "Kayla, let me call you back."

"Is that Keith? He's been calling you since you left his house on your cell. We've been talking for what ten minutes and I heard your phone beep about ten times."

"No, it's not Keith," I lied. "Bye, Kayla. I'll talk to you tomorrow."

"Alright. Call me if you need me."

Before I spoke, I took a deep breath and sipped my mimosa. "Hello."

"Chante, I'm glad to see you made it home safely."

"My heart is in a million pieces, but I don't think you care about that."

"I care."

"Do you really?"

"Why do you think I have been calling you since you left? It seemed like after I called you Lex, you didn't hear anything else I said. I said I was sorry. I asked you to leave your stuff at the door and not to leave. But I guess you didn't hear any of that."

"Keith, I heard what I needed to hear."

"Why did you run out of here like that? We could've talked about it."

"Keith, you called me another bitch's name. What is there to talk about? Did I ever once call you a name that wasn't yours?"

"No but you fucked somebody else although that was something light. What really hurt me was you killed my baby, and you lied."

"So what are we even now?" I screamed.

"Chante, calm down. I didn't call you to argue."

"What did you call me for?"

"Do you know this is our first argument? We have had sex, made a baby, was engaged, and broke up, yet this is our very first argument."

"Is that so?" Now was not the time for Keith to be taking note of the things we had or had not done.

"What you doing?" Keith asked changing the subject.

"Taking a bath."

"Oh I got you stressing like that?"

"Yes, you do."

He laughed. I closed my eyes and listened to him laugh.

"What are you doing?" I asked.

"Driving to my girl's house."

"Keith, look I can't take this. I love you and you know that. I want to be with you, and you also know that. But I cannot be your friend if I am not your lover. What kind of woman do you think I am? Do you think I allow any ole body to come in to the palace? Do you think that because we had sex this morning that we are cool, and you can claim Alexis as your woman, and me and you are going to be friends?" I stood up, wrapping myself in a towel.

"Chante, I love you, too. And I am on my way to your house. Will my key still fit in your lock or have you changed them on me?"